FOUR-CORNERED CIRCLE

Marie and Louise are twin sisters. They've always been close, but now Marie is on the brink of huge success as a children's author, Louise can't help feeling a stab of – what? Not jealousy, exactly, more irritation at her own situation: divorced and drifting. Then there are the unwelcome stirrings that Marie's rakishly handsome husband, Leif, sparks within her... When tragedy strikes, Louise must decide how far she will go to protect her sister – and their whole family. A gripping story of relationships, family – and the dark secrets that can test their limits...

FOUR-CORNERED CIRCLE

Four-Cornered Circle

by

Jon Cleary

Magna Large Print Books
Long Preston, North Yorkshire,
BD23 4ND, England.

British Library Cataloguing in Publication Data.

Cleary, Jon
    Four-cornered circle.

        A catalogue record of this book is
        available from the British Library

        ISBN   978-0-7505-2931-0

First published in Australia in 2007 by
HarperCollinsPublishers Australia Pty Limited

Copyright © Sundowner Productions Pty Limited 2007

Cover illustration © www.britainonview.com

Published in Large Print 2008 by arrangement with
Jon Cleary, care of Curtis Brown

Magna Large Print is an imprint of Library Magna Books Ltd.

Printed and bound in Great Britain by
T.J. (International) Ltd., Cornwall, PL28 8RW

For Cate

Chapter One

1

Louise Fernandez had not changed her name when the divorce came through. Partly because it was too much trouble, changing everything back into her maiden name. Mainly, however, because Micklethwaite was not exactly a clarion call back to single status.

Her mother had always told her it was a proud old English name going back centuries; which was where Louise, even as a child, had thought it should have remained. So Louise Fernandez she still was, even though she and Joe had been divorced for two years. She wore the name like a comfortable coat.

She was dark-haired, worn short to show off the shape of her head; had dark brown eyes which suggested to some people that she had Latin ancestry; which upset her mother, only three generations removed from West Yorkshire, not a hotbed of Latin breeding. She was tall, elegant and only a brushstroke shy of being beautiful. She had high cheekbones and a jawline that ran down to the soft cleft in her chin. Her lips were full, almost a razzberry at collagen, and her teeth pale creamy rather than dazzlingly white. She was the ideal custodian of the Chapelli counter at Dampiers.

Dampiers had begun in 1860 as a Select Emporium for Gentlewomen, a small store that had grown till it now occupied half a block. The Dampiers were long gone and it was now a public company run by male directors who didn't believe there had ever been, nor ever would be, gentlewomen. But they knew who spent the money and so the store was designed for women.

The ground floor was vast enough to have accommodated trains or buses. Instead, there was a maze of glass counters, banks of flowers, a Wurlitzer organ and four huge chandeliers that, myth had it, had hung in a palace in St Petersburg. The Chapelli counter was in one corner, but not in relegation; rather, as a reminder that it, like Bulgari and other aristocrats, was not there for the hoi-polloi. In the last twenty years the fashion aristocrats from abroad had discovered that the Sydney natives, though they might not yet have class, had money. Louise, like an aristocratic spruiker, was there to encourage the natives.

'My dear Miss Fernandez–' He was not a local, but from Kuala Lumpur, rich and sultan-like in his impression of himself. He came to Sydney twice a year and always came to Dampiers to outfit himself and his never-seen wife in jewellery, perfume and other necessities. If his wife ever wore the amount of jewellery and perfume he supposedly took home for her, Louise figured she would never get out of bed, burdened by gold, pearls and enough perfume to have drugged her and called for forensic examination. 'My wife needs a new watch, something delicate–'

Louise unlocked the display case and took out the latest sample. Chapelli had been making watches since men (and women) had decided they had to carry time with them. 'There, Mr Marenda. So delicate I don't know how they squeeze time into it–'

'What a wonderful description!' He was as oily as butter that had gone off.

She poured the cream of her smile over him as if he were a pudding; which he resembled. She had learnt how to manage men – well, maybe not Joe, but the male

11

customers at Dampiers. Men, she had come to know, thought women's humour was accidental; someone like Joan Rivers, not accidental, should be locked up. But the smile and the right amount of flattery kept up her sales figures, which increased her bonus, which kept her in good humour, if not humorous. She never attempted the smile and flattery on women customers. Most of the women who came to the Chapelli counter with their own money were lionesses and she had never been a lion tamer.

'I'll take it–' Then *he* smiled, twenty thousand dollars worth of dentistry. He was as obvious as a billboard, but the rich can afford to be obvious. 'Would you care to have dinner with me this evening?'

'Oh, what a pity! My partner and I are going to the ballet–' Joe still had his uses, though he might not be aware of them.

The smile was reduced to a couple of thousand dollars worth. 'Well, maybe next time. Now what else do I want–'

The would-be sultan paid for everything with a cheque drawn on a Sydney bank; Louise guessed that he didn't want his wife coming across his credit card statement and asking questions. Credit cards had their uses, but they could be dangerous weapons if they fell into the wrong hands, such as those of wives. Louise had half-a-dozen regular clients, from Asia and the Philippines, who had Sydney bank accounts. Mr Marenda asked for his purchases to be sent to his hotel, gave her a ten-thousand-dollar smile, and left. It had been a good morning for the Chapelli counter and Louise didn't care what the rest of the day might bring.

At lunchtime it brought her twin sister. Marie (pronounced Ma-*ree* and don't you forget it) was not an identical twin, but close. She was slightly shorter than Louise, as if waiting for the later delivery at birth had worn her down; she was plumper, though nowhere near fat. She was pretty rather than beautiful, but cameras liked her, in the way that a lens sometimes sees something that the eye has missed. She was not elegant, always running too fast for such indulgence. They had been close as children and even as teenagers; then currents had pulled them apart and now they were just sisters, not twins. Marie had a husband, still attached, and two children, girls aged six and eight, who thought their Aunt Louise was chill. Which, the aunt hoped, was a superlative of cool.

'I'll buy you lunch!' said Marie, who sometimes spoke in gasps, as if she had just run up a hill. There was no physical reason for the gasps, since she was never short of breath or words. 'I think I'm going to be rich!'

'You've won the lottery?'

'No, better than that!'

Louise turned over the counter to Mira, an attractive 20-year-old who was on the lookout for a millionaire, husband or lover, it didn't matter which, she said, and she could find no better watch-tower than the Chapelli counter. Predatory women, like military commanders, choose their terrain carefully.

'Rich men have less time for morals than poor men,' she had once told Louise. 'My mother always said that.'

Louise had wondered at Mira's mother's experience of rich men, but hadn't queried it. 'Just don't be immoral on the Chapelli counter.'

Louise and Marie went down to the café on the lower ground floor. The space was as huge as that of the ground floor; the counters were a sea of glass; butcher's aprons, white smocks, chef's hats were everywhere. This was Chapelli reduced to comestibles: fish, meat, cheeses, cakes instead of jewellery and watches. The food hall had been designed to rival those of Harrods and Fortnum & Mason in London; competition was everything, even at a million or two paces. The café was to one side, a retreat after burdening oneself with shopping. It was still early for lunch and Louise and Marie found a table where they were not surrounded by listening-posts. Sudden wealth, if that was what Marie had achieved, should not be broadcast.

Louise ordered a prawn salad and Marie a crab-and-avocado sandwich. They had always been good eaters, fortunate in that the calories didn't turn into fat. Louise peeled a prawn with elegance, as if taking off a brassiere leisurely, then said, 'So how are you going to be rich?'

Marie looked around her, as if to be re-assured that she would not be overheard; then she leaned forward: 'My new book! I've just come from my publishers–' She was not an elegant eater; she devoured the sandwich as if she were starving. She munched, swallowed while Louise waited patiently, then went on, 'They've already sold it in the States and the UK and they've got foreign publishers making offers. If everything pans out, the advances will start rolling in! This morning they told me it's been optioned for a kids' TV movie.' She took another bite of her sandwich, swallowed and gave another gasp: 'It's fantastic, Lou!'

Louise felt no envy or jealousy. She was capable of mean feelings, but not towards Marie: 'Why have you kept all this so – so quiet for so long?'

'I didn't dare think it could all come off–' She had given up gasping; her voice was soft, as if wondering. 'My first two books, the sales were so-so, hardly worth the time I spent on them. I really wrote them for Brigid and Rosie...'

The café had begun to fill up, people coming in for lunch, unexcited, no thoughts of sudden wealth. Louise looked about her, then back at Marie:

'How does Leif think about it all?' Leif was Marie's husband, a man built to appreciate success. He worked for the State government, where success was manufactured every day, even if out of smoke.

'He knows about the US and UK offers, but he doesn't know yet about the TV deal. Or the foreign rights–'

'How do you feel about it?' Louise peeled another prawn, took a sip of the glass of white wine she had ordered. 'Other than being out of breath?'

'I don't know – yet. Thrilled, I guess. Trying

not to dream too much. There have been plenty of authors who were one-book successes. And kids' literature is chockablock with authors – I'm waiting for Elmore Leonard and James Ellroy to write a kids' book... Anyhow, I still think of myself as a mum who just writes. And a wife,' she added.

'You always wanted to be a writer–'

'Sure.' There had been the short stories sent off to magazines and never acknowledged. There had been four chapters of an autobiographical novel that had petered out because life itself, at twenty, had suddenly had more appeal. 'But a husband and kids...' She shrugged, but not as if they were a burden.

'How do the kids feel? Rosie and Brigid?'

'I haven't told them yet – I don't think they'd understand, I mean about all the money coming in. I wouldn't *want* them to understand, not at their age. I've read them bits of the book and they said they liked it. But it's for older kids.'

'What's it about that it's got everyone wanting to publish it?'

'I honestly don't know. Maybe it's a reaction to all the fantasy that's around.' She knew that the public's taste in books was as unpredictable as the stock market's boom or bust. Who would have predicted that Dan Brown's *The Da Vinci Code* would have become the world-beater that it had? Or that, closer to her own field, Harry Potter would rule the world?

'It's about some schoolkids, 12-year-olds, who decide to hold up a bank to get back 22 dollars and 95 cents that the bank owes one of them. They're in the bank, in balaclavas and toy guns, when real bandits come in. They hold up the bank, kidnap the kids and it goes from there...'

Louise finished her prawn salad, sipped the last of her wine and ordered a coffee. 'Are you going to let the money go to your head?'

'I love you, Lou, but sometimes you can be a real pain in the bum. Why would I let it go to my head? I said I'm going to be rich, but I was exaggerating – this is the book trade, not IT or whatever those kids make their money in. There'll be money to spare, but that'll be the extent of it. You're not envious, are you?'

'You, too, can be a pain in the bum, asking a question like that. No, of course I'm not. Do you want me to give you a hug right out here in the open?'

'Save it for later–' Marie was looking

through her handbag. It was half the size of a chaffbag and was a leatherbound rubbish dump. She had always been the untidy one of them: zipper undone, shoes never cleaned, bed half-made. 'Bugger! I've left my credit card at home – I remember now, it was on the dressing-table. Can you pay for lunch? I'll owe you–'

'God, you're the limit! I've been paying ever since we were in nappies...' She took out her credit card, the weapon of mass attraction, then said quietly, as if the thought had only just occurred to her, 'Mar, how are things between you and Leif?'

'Okay–' Marie didn't seem surprised by the question. In their single days they had discussed men as they might fashion: no secrets, as if warning each other against dangers. 'You know what he's like. He's a great lover and he loves the girls, but he's – is feckless the word?'

Louise had asked the question and been instantly sorry: she had no right to query her sister's married life. 'I dunno. You're the writer.'

'Well, maybe not feckless. Directionless. No direction. Everything has come so easy for him – including me, I just fell into his lap. I don't know how he holds on to his job, except that I know he's good at it.' Leif Johnson was the senior PR man for a minor government minister, part of the regiment of minders that politicians now seemed to need. 'Popularity, I guess. Everybody loves him, from his boss down to the tea-lady.'

I'm half in love with him myself, thought Louise.

'Good luck with the book. Bring your credit card next time.'

2

Leif Johnson had classical Nordic looks; one half-expected a horned helmet on his blond head and a longboat beached behind him. But his original family had left Scandinavia around the time of the Vikings. Family legend, which too often is fiction more than fact, had it that an ancestor had been with Leif Erickson on his way to Vinland, but got wrecked on the rocky shores of Eire, where the Celts soon knocked off the horned helmets and told them Celtic jokes that the Johanssens never understood. Johanssen became Johnson and blond hair turned to dark manes. Centuries passed, then a branch of the family came to Australia, fleeing the potato famine of the mid-nineteenth century, and by then most of the males had names such as Paddy and Liam and Sean. Then a white-headed baby had been born, much to the suspicion of some of the relatives, and the kid, when he was old enough to respond to a name, had found that he was Leif. He grew into a 192-centimetre giant, a muscular young man; he played rugby at university, graduated with a first-class degree, laid girls by the furlong. Then he had fallen in love with Marie Micklethwaite and they were married within a month. He had turned out to be a Viking without longboat or paddle. Still, as everyone said, everyone loved him. Including Leif himself.

'I know I'm conceited,' he would say and everyone would protest, no, no, you're not, you're modest in admitting you're conceited. And he would agree with them, smiling at them and hugging them like a Viking turned local politician.

'What on earth have you done to your hair?' asked Louise. She had noticed the odd fashion over the past couple of years, but none of the men of her acquaintance had adopted it. Till now.

'Lou, it's called arrayed disarray. The side part, the brushback, the mullet, are all passé.' His hair stood up in isolated shoots, like cornstalks badly harvested.

'What do they do to get the effect? Shove hot tongs up your bum?'

'No, they do that only with gays.' He was homophobic and would never change; so Louise never mentioned the one or two gay men she occasionally went out with. 'What I like about you, Lou, is your lady-like vulgarity.'

'It's a natural gift.'

They were at a party thrown by Marie's publishers to launch her new book. A reception room at the Park Hyatt had been booked and it was chockablock with guests, 98 per cent of whom were hoping to be taken for celebrities. Nine out of ten of the women were long-haired blondes, clones of each other and seemingly unaware of the fact. Louise, with her short dark hair, looked foreign, someone with a temporary visa. Paparazzi were on the prowl and smiles, aimed at cameras, lit up the big room like a barrage of gun flashes. Few, if any, had read a children's book in the last fifteen or twenty years, but hey, it was a party...

'Why are parties thrown?' asked Leif. 'Why aren't they hurled or slung?'

'I've been looking at you circulating. You

love yourself, don't you?'

He smiled, not hurt; they had been fencing like this for years. They were standing in a window alcove, Circular Quay and the Opera House a backdrop to them. To their right a wall of lights was the beginning of the central business district, or the CBD, as it was now known, since initials had taken over the world. Each of them had a drink in hand; the publishers, overcome with the prospects ahead, had laid on champagne like tapwater. The fact that it was domestic bubbly and not French was not a sign of parsimony but of patriotism. The Prime Minister was always telling the voters it was un-Australian to be un-Australian.

'Lou, it's all façade. I'm as unsure of myself as the rest of you–' He looked around the throng, who showed no sign of lack of confidence.

'A PR man unsure of himself?'

He smiled again; he was armour-plated, which a PR man had to be. 'Lou, why can't we shake hands and be friends? You're my wife's sister, my kids' favourite aunt. I'm not trying to seduce you–'

You could if you tried. She had pondered, conscience-stricken, as to why she wanted him. There was, of course, the physical attraction; and Marie had said, only a few days ago, that he was a wonderful lover. But was that all she wanted of a man, physical attraction and technique in bed? Double-cross the sister she loved for *that?*

She put out her hand and he took it. 'Okay, Leif – friends. But don't try to impress me, okay? As you said, I'm your wife's sister and your kids' aunt.'

'What else and what more?' But then, all of a sudden, he was looking at her as if seeing her for the first time, or in a new light. It was just for the moment, then he smiled and kissed her cheek.

'Watch it,' said a voice. 'That's my ex-wife.'

Joe Fernandez had arrived, sliding into the gathering without disruption, at home anywhere like a career diplomat or a professional conman. Of which he was neither. Joe was average: average build, average height, average looks. Except for his eyes: they were dark and thoughtful, kind and shrewd. He looked at the world from every angle, but one never knew what he thought. People might take advantage of Joe Fernandez, but only at the point of a gun or a writ. He was a suburban solicitor with his own practice and no aspiration for more recognition, more money, more influence. Louise had loved him, but something, she wasn't sure what, maybe his lack of ambition for his talent, had happened. They had slid apart like a warm ice-floe breaking up. The miscarriage hadn't helped.

Joe kissed her on the cheek and shook hands with Leif. The two brothers-in-law got on well together; like two gorillas, Louise once said, one inside the cage, the other outside.

'So we're going to have a celebrity in the family?' Joe occasionally talked as if he still belonged. 'Where is she?'

'Over there, where the crowd is thickest,' said Leif and looked suddenly proud of Marie. And not as if he created her. *Thank God*, thought Louise, *he's not jealous of her*. 'Rosie and Brigid curtsey now every time she passes them. I wish your dad was here to enjoy it,' he said to Louise. 'And your mum.'

'Dad's not well enough to stand up at cocktail parties. And he'd hate being made a fuss of if he were sitting down.'

'I called him the other day–' Joe was still part of the family, at least as far as Matt Micklethwaite was concerned. 'He says the retirement village is like a bloody holiday camp. They wanted him to take up ballroom dancing, him with his arthritis. He's bloody near crippled with it.'

'Mum would have had the time of her life,' said Louise. Her mother, a ball of fire, had been dead three years, going suddenly without warning like a puff of smoke. 'She'd have been autographing the books for Marie, flogging them in the street–'

'I think I'll go over and stand in the author's warm glow,' said Leif and made his way across the crowded room to the star of the evening. On his way he was stopped several times, each time by a woman. One of them was a celebrity, a catwalk supermodel who, it was said, would go to the opening of a grave. She had cheekbones like scalpels, a flat chest, skeletal arms and legs, and collagen-enhanced lips in the gauntly beautiful face like a baby's teething-ring.

'Her lips are thicker than her legs,' said Louise.

'Meow,' said Joe. 'But he's giving her the brush-off, in the nicest possible way. Why do I like him while I hate him?'

'Me, too,' said Louise and took a glass from the tray of a passing waiter and gave it to Joe. 'How's business?'

He looked at her, then out the window. The shell of the Opera House glowed like a sculpted iceberg; a river-cat slid out from a wharf like a huge crocodile. He loved this city, but chose to live and work in its suburbs. Yet Louise had never been sure he did it for safety's sake.

He looked back at her. There was always a slight constraint when they were together, but it wasn't uncomfortable. Living together, sleeping together, weaves a net that doesn't always fray. 'It's okay. People keep dying, that's one figure that never changes. I drew up seven wills last week. Divorces keep happening, more regularly–' He paused there, as if he had for the moment forgotten their own and only now remembered it. Then he went on, 'And people keep committing crimes and wanting mortgages and wanting to sue. That's the bit that worries me. Litigation is becoming too fashionable, there are more ambulance-chasers than there are ambulances. How's it with you?'

'I just shake my head... We're in what they're calling a mild recession, profits are down at Dampiers, yet I'm still selling four- and five-thousand-dollar watches and perfume at two hundred dollars an ounce.'

'You smell pretty good. How much did that cost?'

'I put it on lay-by a drop at a time. How's

your love life?'

'I thought we'd agreed never to discuss that?'

'I'm sorry. I'm just in a bad mood tonight–' She had felt it growing, like a cold coming on.

He looked at her, the thoughtful eyes now critical. 'You're not jealous of Marie, are you?'

'Of course I'm not! God, Joe, you can get under my skin–'

'Get off the boil. Jealousy is a natural thing–'

'It isn't with me!' *I'm starting to sound shrill.* 'Was I ever jealous of you?'

'No. No, I don't think you were... Come on, let's go over while I congratulate the author, then I'll take you to dinner downstairs.'

She hesitated, then nodded. 'Why are you always so bloody sympathetic?'

'Solicitous, not sympathetic. That's what solicitors are for. Come on.'

He took her by the hand and they swam through the breakers of the crowd, blinded by the smiles looking for the paparazzi. Both of them were strangers here and no one took any notice of them. They came to Marie, bright-eyed and wide-smiling. Two-

and-a-half glasses into the champagne, she glowed like a small beacon; but her smile was the genuine article, coming from deep inside her. Joe kissed her on the cheek and she responded with a fierce hug. They had always been the best of in-laws and she had done her interfering best, until told by Louise to lay off, to keep her sister and Joe together. 'Oh, Joe, just the man I wanted to see! They tell me I'm going to need a lawyer–'

'Any time, love. Where can I get a copy of the book?'

'Right here! Right here!' She turned and snatched two copies of the book from a display table. 'You want me to autograph it? You too, Lou?'

'Mar, we're *family*, remember? I'll autograph Joe's and he can autograph mine.' Then Louise suddenly heard the sourness in her voice and she smiled, stretching her face. 'Another time, Mar. Just go on enjoying tonight.' She was aware of Joe's thoughtful eyes on her. 'Every minute of it!'

'I'm busting to get out of here!' Then Marie lowered her voice, looked conspiratorial, as if they would understand. 'Leif and I have booked a room here for the night – I might as well splash the wealth! One of the girls from his office is babysitting–' She kissed them both again; she had been kissing cheeks all evening. Joe, who read the lighter side of history, said osculation had never been so popular. 'Talk to me tomorrow, Joe. You too, Lou–'

Louise and Joe made their way through the crowd towards the lifts. The blondes looked at Louise and asked– 'Who's she? Must be a foreigner. Maybe a New Zealander, they're all dark-haired, aren't they?' Nobody recognized her; nobody at literary parties was a customer at the Chapelli counter.

Going down in the lift, the two of them alone, Joe said, 'I couldn't be happier for her. I hope Leif is, too.'

Louise looked sideways at him. 'What makes you say that?'

Joe took his time: 'All his life, I'd say, he's wanted to be a success. He's just never had the stamina. He's got all the talent, he just gets in his own way. He spends all his time being popular.'

'You sound envious–' Then she smiled and took his hand. 'Sorry. We've both sounded envious tonight.'

'Someone once said, envy is a kind of praise. It was probably a Frenchman, they're good at aphorisms. Let's say we're praising

30

him. It'll make us feel better.'

'Do you give that kind of advice to your clients?'

'Only for a fee.'

He took her arm as the lift came to the ground floor. She was as tall as he in her high heels, but he always gave her the impression of being shorter. She liked her tallness, but was thankful she was not a basketballer's height. She looked at some of those giantesses and imagined someone like Joe clambering over them like a mountaineer. She had been thankful that Joe had never been a clamberer in bed. The first boy she had gone to bed with had been like that, shorn only of climbing boots and pitons.

'What are you smiling at?' asked Joe.

'Nothing,' she said and gave him a smile all for himself.

Joe was a quiet, unassertive man, but he always managed to get a good table in a restaurant. As tonight, a window table.

'How do you always manage it?' Louise asked, remembering.

'I booked on my way in,' said Joe. 'Flattery always helps, too. I told the girl on the desk I liked her hair.'

'Did she believe you? That's something new, isn't it? You learning to flatter?' Then

31

she said, still in good humour, 'You were sure I'd come to dinner?'

'You or someone else.' He grinned, never a wide grin, always thin, as if he were trying to hide his teeth, which were even and bright white. 'Relax.'

Sometimes, like a slight nervous tremor, there was a stirring inside her for him, the Joe of ten years ago. It was partly sexual, partly the sense of reliance: he had been *there*. Something tonight (Marie's success? Leif?) had unsettled her and now here was Joe, the anchor of long ago. A drag, sometimes, like an anchor; but *there*. Or rather now, *here*.

'How's your appetite?'

'Ravenous.' *God, listen to me! Like the women in an Almódovar movie. If I keep on like this I'm going to take him home to bed. And be sorry in the morning.* One-night stands were shipwrecks for divorced couples. She had heard Joe himself say that when they had still been together and he was handling a divorce case that kept going off course. 'I'd like a steak–'

'Two,' Joe told the waiter. 'And would you mind asking the chef if he'd do onions with mine?'

'He's French, sir. He'll be delighted.'

The waiter went away and Louise said, 'I

32

bet you knew the chef was French.'

He shook his head. 'No, the waiter was smart. I always thought steak-and-onions was an Aussie dish. We never had it at home. Mum always cooked Spanish.'

His parents, socialists both, having suffered General Franco all their lives, fled Spain the year before El Caudillo died, a major error of timing and judgement. Hernando Fernandez had been a second-string picador, trained for nothing else. There had been little or no demand for picadors in Sydney, though a newspaper leader-writer had suggested they could be used to gee-up politicians. Hernando, on the principle that he was used to the sight of blood, got a job in an abattoir on the edge of the city. Joe had been three years old when the family of three landed in Australia and he had taken to his new country like an indigene. His parents, no longer socialists nor bloodstained, now lived in a small cottage on the Central Coast, not far from the retirement village where Matt Micklethwaite suffered the rigors of arthritis and over-enthusiastic carers. They got together occasionally when Hernando would regale Matt, a rugby league fan, with stories of a far gorier sport. Isabella Fernandez watched Spanish movies on Foxtel and wondered what she had missed in her youth, when sin had been the second-biggest crime after sedition. She would have been shocked to learn that her ex-daughter-in-law watched the same movies with relish and revived memories.

Louise, taking the bit between her teeth, said, 'Joe, what happened to us?'

'I dunno, love.' He looked at his wine, as if into a crystal ball. He always took his time about opinions; bullfighters, he had once told her, took their time so they would survive. 'If we had stayed together, we might have killed each other. Slowly. Or not, I dunno. It happens – I see it every week. Couples coming to my office, jumping to get apart before they start tearing each other to pieces. I saw some figures the other day. Forty per cent of today's marriages will end in divorce before their silver anniversaries. Maybe much earlier.'

'Do you ever get depressed by your work?' She had never asked him that before. But then she had been happy with him, selfish in what she had.

'Often. Lawyers weren't created to spread good news. More wine?'

'Just a little – I've had more than enough tonight.'

'Relax, Lou. I've got no designs on your virginity. Born again, that is.' He grinned again. He had read her mind; or her doubts. 'How's work? People still buying Chapelli as if they were giveaways?'

'At the Chapelli level, there'll always be people with money to spare. I once read that money never runs out, it just shifts like – what do they call 'em – tectonic plates.'

'You should've been an economist. Do you ever get bored?' The thoughtful look again, probing this time. 'With life in general, I mean.'

Of course she did. All her life there had been someone close to her: her twin, her parents, Joe himself. She had never prepared herself for loneliness and that was where boredom could grow. She fenced: 'Do you?'

'No. But I get depressed sometimes. At what people do to each other.'

She picked up her copy of Marie's book. 'I'll read this, see if Marie is optimistic about kids.'

'I'm always optimistic about *them...*'

She remembered his huge disappointment when she had miscarried.

Then their steak-and-onions arrived.

Louise was in bed reading:

Robbing a bank is a pretty crummy idea for a school project, but all we were trying to do was to get back Rachel's $22.95...

My name is Barney Guinness. My father, who owns a wine and spirits shop, persuaded my dumb mother to christen me Johnny Walker St Bernard Shiraz Guinness. I'm not kidding. Actually, my mother isn't dumb. She's a very nice lady, sometimes, and she had a pretty hard time delivering me. Honestly, that's what they call it. Delivering. As if your mother is a courier from DHL or Federal Express or something. Anyhow, when I was delivered, unwrapped, she told my dad, 'Call him what you like, but don't call me.' Then she went to sleep for two whole days. I don't know who fed me, probably a St Bernard. When she woke up she called me Barney.

I go to what they call an Opportunity School. It's in Sydney, in what they call the inner city, don't ask me why. Kids from all over come to it and we're supposed to be extra-brainy, but sometimes I dunno. Like the bank job...

Well, anyway, there was Rachel Finkelberg this day in the playground at recess. Doing her usual thing – dancing a flamenco. You know, that Spanish dance, all the stamping of the feet, snapping the fingers, and Rachel shouting, 'Oi vay!'

'Rach,' I said, 'for Pete's sake, it's olé! *Even I know that.'*

'Out in Bellevue Hill it isn't.' That's where she lives. Her parents are Jewish Spanish or something.

'Well, for Pete's sake, change to something else. Try ballroom dancing.'

'You wanna be my partner?'

'You're kidding.' I couldn't dance on hot sand.

So she changes. Irish dancing. Honestly. All that bloody clatter of boots again and her arms tight down her sides like she's in a straitjacket. No wonder so many Irish, like my dad, left home, everybody dancing as if they're in a crowded bus. They must be short of space in Ireland.

'Rachel!'

So she kicks off her shoes and, you won't believe this, starts a soft-shoe shuffle, I think they call it, whistling something through the gap in her teeth. She's not my girlfriend, otherwise I'd give her away.

After a while she stops, sits down and looks pretty unhappy. I'm not the softest guy around, so my mother tells me, but I said, 'What's biting you, Rach?'

'The bank over there,' she says and nods.

Out in front of our school there is a small park. Well, not a park. A reserve; though I dunno what it's reserved for. It's been there a thousand years or that's what you'd think if you listened to Mrs Drufrock, our principal. She's a nut on history, bores you blind with dates on who done what to who and where. History, my dad says, is the biggest fairy story of all time. Anyhow, on the other side of the reserve there is a row of shops and this bank.

'What about it?'

'They're trying to rob me. I've got 22 dollars 95 cents in my account over there. I want to take it out, I was gunna buy my mum a Mother's Day present, and they said I owed 19 dollars and 74 cent in bank fees.'

'Can they do that?'

'I dunno. The bank manager's name is Mr Kelly. Probably a relation of Ned Kelly.'

'Ned Kelly robbed banks, he didn't manage them.'

'What's going on?'

That was Bird the Nerd. She's a computer whiz and reckons when she grows up she's going to buy Microsoft from Bill Gates. Her real name is Birdsong Maguire. Her mum is what they used to call a hippie, gets around in loopy dresses and wears a band round her head. My dad says *the effect is spoiled by the fact that Mrs Maguire has more money than Bill Gates, the band round her head has pearls or diamonds or something on it and she drives a, I'm not kidding, Bentley 4WD the size of a battleship. Honestly. There are seven other mums, including mine, who have insurance claims against her for the dents she has put in their cars when she's parking the 4WD. Bird is embarrassed by her, but won't leave home. Staying for the money, I guess.*

We explained what had happened to Rachel's $22.95 and Bird said, 'I could put a virus in their computers.' And she could, too. My dad says the CIA already have their eye on her. Probably Bill Gates has too.

'What's going on? A virus in what computer?'

That was Darky Bindinjarra, one of three Aboriginal kids in the school and my best mate. The first time I took him home I said to Mum, 'This is Darky', and she belted me across the back of my head. She's an anti-racist liberal feminist conservationist and she belts me across the head every time I insult a whale. When she was at university she was too late to be burning her bra, but she tossed it away anyway and wore none (disgusting) and must have been a real pain in the neck.

'What's your name?' she asks Darky. Incidentally, he calls me Whitey or Pale Bum.

39

'Algernon.'

Honestly. That's his name – Algernon Bindin-jarra. And I complain about St Bernard.

'Would you like something?' she said and gave him carrot cake and herbal tea. She was out of witchetty grubs, I guess.

Later Darky said to me, 'Is this what your mum thinks us Kooris eat and drink? Would she like to be a Koori?'

Fat chance. I once heard my mother and father having sex (disgusting) and she was yelling, 'Do you like me blonde and beautiful?' and he was shouting, 'I love you blonde and beautiful!' I think when I get around to having sex, I'll keep my mouth shut...

Louise put down the book. She had no idea whether it would appeal to kids, though she had read that children's authors were now outselling those who wrote for adults. Even as a child she had never had much time for children's books, though she had liked the upside-down wisdom in *Alice in Wonderland*. At twelve, Barney Guinness' age, she had been reading Jilly Cooper and Jackie Collins. In brown-paper covers. She hoped *Barney's Bank Job* would be more than a one-off for Marie.

Joe had brought her home in his BMW saloon (no convertible man, he, no wind in

40

the hair and dark glasses), made no attempt to get out of the car, just leaned across and kissed her on the cheek. She had been tempted to ask him in, wanting sex, but reason had prevailed. One-night stands with a stranger, or a new acquaintance, could be risky, but with an ex-husband they could be a quicksand.

A year ago she had bought a vibrator, but it had proved cold comfort. Bringing herself to orgasm was nowhere near as satisfying as having a lover do it; she was an old-fashioned girl whom the whores of history would have applauded.

In the two years since the divorce there had been two men, both failures, not at sex but at whatever she had been looking for. And, to her chagrin, she could not define exactly what she was looking for. She could imagine her mother berating her for her vagueness; Matt Micklethwaite had been Norah Ames' one and only true love. And Norah had been the same for Matt: Louise could not imagine her father ever thinking of another woman. If they were trying to pair him off with some widow in the retirement village, they would have better luck with the Pope.

Which reminded her. She reached for the remote control on the bedside table and switched on the television. Even when she had been with Joe she had always insisted that the TV set was not to be in the living room; she had not wanted it sitting there while they had visitors, its blank screen inviting the pressing of a button or some male guest asking could they check the cricket or football scores. This main bedroom was large and the set stood in one corner, the window on the world beyond the room's other windows.

A replay of Pope John Paul II's funeral came up on the screen and she looked at it with detachment. She had been a regular at Mass till she was twenty; then, like so many other women she knew, she had fallen away. She was now a twice-a-year Catholic, at Easter and Christmas; she never went to what used to be called Confession and, still with conscience lingering, never took Communion. Now she watched the slow procession of cardinals, resplendent in what Marie, another part-timer, called their party hats and ballgowns. It struck Louise how remarkably well-fed all of them looked: 115 cardinals and 230 chins. She looked at all these celibate old men who decided what women should do with their bodies and once again wondered how the Church, losing priests, nuns and parishioners, would progress, or decline further, under a new Pope. Even Norah, a weekly Massgoer, had stormed at the Church's rejection of women. She, once devout, had come to speak of 'that old men's home in Rome'. The Vatican, of course, had thick walls and deaf ears.

Louise switched channels and got a replay of the wedding of Prince Charles and Camilla Parker Bowles. She smiled at the British upper classes in *their* fancy hats and agreed with Marie and what she had once said: the British upper classes were the world's worst-dressed. They made the cardinals look like fashion stylists. She switched off the set, smug in her colonial elegance.

She got out of bed, went to the bathroom, came back and got into bed again, looked around her. She had little to complain about. When the divorce had come through, there had been a fair property settlement. She had had no wish to stay on in the house they had then owned; nor had Joe. That had been sold and she had bought this two-bedroom flat in Abbotsford with a view of Hen and Chicken Bay. She had her own car now, a Barina; she had never been a car woman wanting a BMW or Nissan sports. She earned $38,000 a year, plus bonuses, and she had shares that Joe had turned over to her. Many women would have thought she was sitting pretty, but the seat was loose and uncomfortable. And she wasn't sure why.

She had had two affairs after she separated from Joe. The first had been an academic who had told her he admired the curve in her lower back. It threw up her pelvis, he said, when she was flat on her back during sexual conjugations (he talked like that). He taught Middle East history and he had told her all the great Eastern houris had had it; as if he had conjugated with them personally. She hadn't appreciated being compared to a houri. Not in Abbotsford, where harems were in short supply and caliphs, if any, wore trainers instead of slippers with curved-up toes.

The second affair had been with an architect, a consummate lover who didn't apply architectural principles. She had thought she was falling in love with him till one day his estranged wife appeared at the Chapelli counter.

'He's told me about you–' She had a soft but firm voice. 'Did you know he's been spending the occasional night with me?'

'No, he didn't. He never mentioned you–'

He had broached the subject of his wife only once and Louise had told him to shut up, she did not want a threesome in bed.

The wife was a well-dressed, good-looking woman who might have been at the counter buying a bottle of Chapelli's *Garden of Eden*, top of the range and with no apple scent. 'I'm going ahead with the divorce. Your name has come up–'

Louise shook her head, glad that Mira was away having coffee and there were no other customers at the counter. 'No – *please*. I don't want that. Do you?'

'No. But if I have to–'

'No.' Louise bit her lip, embarrassed and sorry for the other woman. 'Tell him you've been to see me and that I'm fed up and it's over. Or I'll tell him if you like–'

'No, it'll give me great pleasure.' Then she smiled, put out a gloved hand; she was the sort of woman, Louise noted, who wore gloves. Old-fashioned, yet modern in her approach to divorce. They shook hands and she said, 'Thank you. In a way I don't blame you – he's charming and knows how to chase women. But he's a bastard and you'd have found that out in time. Goodbye.'

And now she turned out the light, as if to hide the tears that were suddenly on her cheeks. It hurt that her last thought before she fell asleep was of Marie and Leif in bed at the Park Hyatt.

Chapter Two

1

It had been a wild night in bed. Once she had let fly with a bugle-call of ecstasy and out on the harbour a late-night ferry had paused, thinking someone had fallen overboard. Leif was her bull, her stallion, her stag, but he could also be amazingly gentle. Marie turned her head to look at him. He was still asleep, his face as serene as that of a child; sometimes, though never telling him, she thought of him as her third child. He needed protection, from himself as much as against the world.

He opened one eye, closed it again in a wink. 'You're still here?'

'I'm paying, remember? Come on, get up.' She slid out of bed, turning her back on him and the temptation to touch him. At home they were never as tempestuous as they had been last night, always conscious of their girls just down the hallway. 'You can go straight to the office, but I've got to get back home. Dinah won't want to be late for work.' Dinah was the girl from Leif's office who had volunteered to babysit for them last night. 'You have breakfast here, I'll go home.'

He rolled over on his back, stretched like an animal coming awake. 'You think of everything. Fresh shirt, fresh underpants – do I have to wear the same tie as yesterday?' He grinned and reached for her, but she stood up and headed for the bathroom. 'Thanks for the night. Will you leave your name and phone number?'

He was under the shower when she was ready to leave. She opened the shower door, stood back so she would not be sprayed and blew him a kiss.

He dropped the soap on the floor of the shower and, grinning, said, 'Pick up the soap?'

'No way. This is no footballers' shower–'

He looked irresistible, standing there naked, shining with water, but temptation had to be resisted. She blew him another kiss, made sure his clothes were laid out on the rumpled bed and left.

Downstairs she paid the bill with her credit card and the desk clerk said, 'Congratulations, Mrs Johnson. I've already got a copy of your book–' She wondered if he had got it for himself; he looked to be just out of high school. 'I hope the reception last night was a success?'

'Couldn't have been more successer–' *What's the matter with me? Get used to being a success.* 'Is there a cab outside?'

'Waiting for you,' he said and for a heady moment she thought she was JK Rowling. Barney Guinness would outshine Harry Potter, all without magical powers. She floated out to the cab, airborne.

The Johnsons lived in a house in Wollstonecraft, supposedly on the Lower North Shore, though seagulls, heading north from the harbour, usually turned back before they got to Wollstonecraft. It was a double-fronted brick house from the twenties of the last century (she still had trouble moving from one century to another). It had no swimming pool (making them socially disadvantaged, said Leif) but a pleasant garden back and front and a double garage at the side. It had a tiled roof, weighed down with a $370,000 mortgage. The Micklethwaites and the Johnsons, parents comfortable, had helped with the purchase, but the mortgage always hung over the place like a tree about to topple. Leif turned a blind eye and a deaf ear to it; debt, he believed, was a natural human condition, like bad skin or haemorrhoids, neither of which plagued him. Marie, on the other hand, indeed on both hands, wore the mortgage like a hairshirt. And now, all of a sudden, it was going to be lifted, cast off.

She got out of the cab, asked the driver to wait. 'How much do I owe you? I want you to take a girl back to town.'

He told her and she gave him the money, plus a ten-dollar tip. He, all the way from Outer Mongolia, new to the job, almost fell out of his seat at the generosity of Aussies. He had not yet learned that Aussies were at the bottom of the tipping scale and that Aussie women were the tightest of the lot. He also didn't know that success had made the generous lady light-headed.

Marie paused inside her front gate and looked at the house, its tiled roof seemingly brighter now that the mortgage was about to be lifted. Even the tibouchina tree, between the path and the driveway and now in fading bloom, like a dying purple explosion, suddenly looked brighter. She wasn't singing as she went up the garden path to the front door, but she did a hop-skip-and-jump up the steps. All that was missing was a 50-piece orchestra.

Dinah Camplin was another blonde (Sydney was starting to look like Stockholm) with a likeable smile and a languid air that suggested she liked leaning against door jambs as if looking for trade. She wore cleavage as a fashion note and Marie would not have given her a thought as a babysitter if either of her children had been a boy (say, one like Barney Guinness). But Rosie and Brigid thought her *fantastic* and asked couldn't Mum and Dad go out again, so they could have Dinah to keep them company.

'We watched *Neighbours* and *The Simpsons* and everything!' thrilled Rosie, too bright to be only six. 'Go out again, Mum–'

'Dinah wouldn't let us see *Desperate Housewives*,' said Brigid, eight going on eighteen.

Dinah smiled. 'They were in bed at 8.30. I read them part of your book... I liked it. I do hope it goes like a bomb–'

'Wrong metaphor, Dinah. Books bomb every week–' She walked out with Dinah to the cab. Blossoms from the tibouchina fell on them as they passed under it, like a blessing. 'Thanks a lot. I'm glad Leif recommended you. The last babysitter we had, I think she'd been a prison warden.'

'Your husband's such a nice man–'

'Do you work under him?' *Whoa, Marie.*

51

Care to rephrase that?

Dinah smiled, but made no comment. 'No, I'm in Complaints. In a government department you get those all the time.'

'Do you do much babysitting?'

'This was the first time. You have such nice girls – I mightn't be so lucky next time.' She got into the front seat of the cab beside the driver: a true-blue Aussie. He looked uncomfortable, as if thinking of Outer Mongolia and customs there. In Ulaanbaatar he had driven a bus and the women had been the worst, most abusive passengers. The lady beside him said to the other, generous lady, 'Enjoy being famous–'

'I'll try–' But the cab had already pulled away and Marie stood there alone on the footpath in the empty street, not a cheer or a handclap to be heard. She looked around her, then smiled wryly. She had a long way to go.

She went inside, changed into slacks and sweater, got the girls ready for school, took them out to the Corolla (six years old and to be replaced by – what? A Jaguar?) and edged the car out of the garage and down the driveway. She was a careful driver, while Leif drove as if on the waiting list for Grand Prix call-up.

'Mum,' said Brigid, 'I liked your book, what Dinah read to us.'

'Thank you.' All critics should be eight years old.

'Do you read dirty books? Jade says her mum does.'

Leif had once brought home the *Kama Sutra* and she had read it and decided she was not going to risk spinal dislocation trying for some of the recommended positions. 'No, I read clean books. When you're older, I'll read you a lovely book called *Little Women.*'

'Urk!' said Rosie and Brigid, and Marie wondered which teacher had tossed Louisa May Alcott out the window. Progressive schools could be too progressive.

She dropped the girls off at the private school they attended, waved to several mums who shouted 'Congratulations!' and gave them what she hoped was a celebrity small-wattage smile. She had always been modest, but now she was learning she had to practise it. As she was getting back into the car she was accosted by Jade's mother. She was a drab, overweight woman whose husband was a notorious drunk and she possibly needed dirty books, as some sort of distraction.

'I'm looking forward to reading your book.'

Possibly as a change of diet from erotica. *'Barney's Wank Job* – what a great title!'

'Yes, isn't it,' said Marie, glad she hadn't thought of it.

She went home, elated again and happy, put the car in the garage, went into the house and was suddenly, inexplicably, empty. She sat down at the kitchen table, still littered with breakfast dishes, cereal packets, honey and jam jars (Dinah, the babysitter, was obviously not a housekeeper), and began to weep.

She wept for almost five minutes, without understanding why. Was it that she had turned a corner and suddenly faced a landscape she did not know? Was she afraid of success? Or that success might prove very short-lived? Or was it that this was what she had longed for, ever since she had been a teenager, and it had come too late? At that she stopped weeping, wiped her eyes and nose and snapped at herself for her selfishness. And for her inflated idea of success: she still had a long way to go, if ever, before she could take it for granted.

She cleared the table, put the dishes in the dishwasher, then went through to make the girls' beds. But stopped in the living room and looked around. It was a comfortable but mixed room, a combination of Leif's taste for the modern and her own taste for an earlier period. Her mother's old upright piano stood against one wall; Norah had been a good pianist but nostalgic for times and songs long gone. She had even played ragtime, to the embarrassment of Marie and Louise, in front of their teenage friends. Rosie had inherited her grandmother's ear for music, but so far, at six, wasn't playing ragtime. Opposite the piano was Leif's CD player with all his choices, most of which didn't appeal to her. On the walls were several paintings, none of which had cost them much; the exception was a Grace Cossington Smith painting of flowers, which had been her mother's and *her* mother's. A small bookcase held some of her mother's choices: Margaret Drabble, Edna O'Brien and Thea Astley. On a shelf below were her father's favourites, Hornblower and other sailors: he loved sea stories, even though he got seasick standing on a wharf. She stood, looking around her as if looking at her life on a cyclorama, and all at once she knew that, whatever the new brought, she was not going to dump the old. There might be an argument with Leif over that, but she would be adamant.

She had finished her housework, was

having a cup of coffee at the kitchen table, when her mobile rang. She had a love-hate relationship towards it. It had once rung while she was in the middle of an orgasm with Leif; she hadn't answered it, the ringing going on and on while she and Leif kept up a faster rhythm. She answered it now: 'Yes?' Should she give her name in case it was an interviewer? 'Marie Johnson.'

'Who else would it be?' said Joe, unimpressed. 'You still getting over last night?'

What part of last night was he referring to? She took the safe option: 'The book launch? I'll survive. My publishers are lining up interviews, the papers and radio and TV.'

'And how are you taking it?' He sounded as if he were in court probing a witness.

'I've just done the housework and I'm now sitting at the kitchen table having a coffee before I do the washing.'

'That's my girl – keep your feet on the ground.'

He was the best male friend she had ever had: *friend* as distinct from *boyfriend*. There was a reassurance about him; a contrast to Leif, though she never admitted that to herself. She had been bitterly upset when Joe and Louise had divorced. She had done everything she could to persuade Louise to try again, only to be told to mind her own business. Vaguely she had begun to see that in the immediate future she might need a rock to cling to, and Joe would always be a rock. She was glad he had called.

'You said you wanted a solicitor – why? Don't you have an agent?'

'Joe, I had three of them approach me last night. But I don't know any of them. I know *you*. My first two books, I let my publishers draw up the contracts – they earned bugger-all, so it didn't matter much. But now...'

'I'm your man, love. What commission do they pay agents?'

'Joe, we're *friends!*'

'Okay, we're friends, less ten per cent. If you're going to earn big money, you'll have to learn there are wolves all around. Better a friendly wolf than a vicious one. I'll be over tonight, around eight, okay?'

'Not tonight, Joe – I'm still exhausted.' For various reasons. She changed the subject: 'How's it with Louise? You looked very matey last night. You took her to dinner.'

'She and I are just friends, no commission. Don't try to make anything more of it. You're a kids' writer, not a romance writer–'

'I just hate to see the two of you un-happy–'

'Mar, lay off. Stop playing Barbara Cartland. We're not unhappy, neither of us–'

'I can hear it in your voice–'

'Oh Christ, you writers!'

But when he hung up she wasn't sure whether he was laughing or crying.

2

'Dad, is Mum gunna be famous?'

'I dunno,' said Leif. 'What's famous?'

'I dunno,' said Rosie. 'Brigid doesn't know, either.'

'Shane Warne's famous,' said Brigid.

'Who's she?' said Rosie.

'I dunno.'

Leif looked across the dinner table at Marie. 'You're going to find it tough to impress these two...' He bit into the lamb cutlet, chewed, then said, 'Have you thought any more about an agent?'

'Yes, I'm going to use Joe–'

'He's not an agent–' He attacked the second cutlet. He enjoyed his food and her cooking and never mentioned the expenses-paid lunches he sat down to. 'Pick your cutlet up in your hand, Rosie, it's easier to eat that way–'

'Well, Joe's the one I'm going to use,' said Marie, chewing on a hand-held cutlet. 'I want someone I *know*. And he's tough and shrewd, you've said so yourself.'

He nodded, almost reluctantly. He and Joe were not friends, but they got on well together and he had been as much upset as Marie when the Fernandezes had broken up. 'Well, yes–'

'Well, yes it is...' She changed the subject: 'I didn't tell you – I liked Dinah. The girls liked her, too.'

'She's fantastic, Dad,' said Brigid. 'Can we have her again?'

'How'd you find her?' asked Marie. 'She said she didn't work for you–'

'I didn't find her. I asked some of the girls in the office if they knew a babysitter – you said you were so unhappy with the last one–'

'Urk!' said Brigid.

'Dinah came to me, said she'd seen you and the girls one day when you came to the office – we were going out for lunch, I think – and she said she'd heard I was looking for a babysitter–'

'I liked her, but she didn't look the sort who'd be offering herself as a babysitter–'

Leif looked at his daughters. 'Did you like her?'

'Fantastic!' said Rosie, limited like most of the population, reporters, commentators, celebrities, in her vocabulary. 'Bring her again!'

'She's light up top,' Leif told Marie. 'She'd have trouble having a headache.'

'She's fantastic,' said Brigid, and her father looked along the table at their mother, shrugged and gave up.

Later, after she had showered the girls and put them to bed, Marie came into the living room and dropped into a chair opposite Leif. The TV was switched off and he was making notes for a speech he had to write for his minister.

'You should be doing this,' he said. 'It's a fairytale he wants.'

'I'm exhausted! I think I'll be a successful author and go away to a health camp–'

'I'll come with you.' He put down his scribble pad. He was adept with words and often made his minister sound better-educated and wittier than that gentleman would ever be on his own. 'We'll find a babysitter who can move in for a few days...' He looked at her with concern. 'Is it proving too much, honey?'

'Honey? Where'd you get that from?'

'I dunno.' He frowned, as if he had been

caught swearing in front of the children. 'Okay. Sweetheart – that better?'

'It'll do... No, it's not proving too much. It's just that– I dunno, the future might prove too much–'

'Sweetheart, it's only one book so far. I'm not putting you down–'

'I could be a nine day wonder?' Though she had never known what a nine day wonder was. She must look it up.

'Sweetheart, one thing you learn as a PR man is, forget the future. If you worried about that, you'd never get anything written or promoted. There's only the present, which, even as I've said it, is already the past.'

'Well, at the present, no matter how long it lasts, I haven't a clue what I'm going to write next. So I think we'd better sit down and start thinking about how we're going to save our windfall and not spend it... What's the matter?'

'Well, I was thinking, I dunno, why couldn't we have a trip overseas? I've got leave coming up. London and Paris...'

'Taking Rosie and Brigid? You think I want to drag them around London and Paris while you – where would you be?'

'I'd be there with you, *parlez-vousing* with

the kids–'

'You're out of your mind.' She was a dreamer, but she could be very practical at times. 'People who can afford a nanny do that sort of thing. What do we do? Take Dinah, the fantastic babysitter?'

'We wouldn't want her along–'

'The first thing we do with the money is pay off the mortgage–'

He slapped a hand against the arm of the lounge where he sat. 'Oh for Crissake, let's enjoy the – the windfall. The bank's not going to foreclose on us – not now they know you're in the money. They'll be offering us new loans – banks never turn their backs on someone else's windfall–'

They had been married nine years. They were not always in harmony, but they had always kept their arguments low-key, protecting the children from them. The arguments invariably were about money. They were always about his attitude towards it: money had been invented to be spent, not saved. Money, as coinage, he would tell her, had been invented seven centuries before Christ and, he would also tell her, sure as hell hadn't gone into savings accounts. She was not thrifty, but she was not profligate.

'No. We spend it my way–' And knew she

sounded like a selfish shrew. But knew, too, that he would never change, always living for the moment, let the future look after itself.

He stared at her for a long moment, then he went back to his scribble pad, dreaming up words as empty as he seemed to think his own future was. She looked across at him, wondering why love at times had so many rough edges to it.

They went to bed cool as strangers. It was nothing like last night had been. Once she did cry out in her sleep, but it was muffled and she didn't hear it nor did he.

During the night a wind sprang up and out in the front garden the tibouchina tree lost the last of its blossoms.

Chapter Three

1

Joe Fernandez was interviewing a client:

'She's been to bed with fifteen fellers? What was it, a rugby team?'

He was in his office, a large comfortable room that had once been a family's drawing-room. One wall, where nineteenth-century paintings had once hung, was now covered with bookshelves, the decoration now books with titles that would excite only lawyers. Deep windows were behind Joe and out in the large rear garden shrubs and a magnolia tree writhed in the wind. It was a comforting room, at least for Joe Fernandez.

Harold Pincole was a large man: large body, large face and head, large eyebrows that gave him the appearance of always being surprised. He was the chief engineer for a large cargo carrier and spent three or four months at a time at sea. He claimed to be a man of infinite patience, but his emotional measuring skills were doubted by Joe.

'There were five rugby blokes. And a cricketer and a basketball player. The others are a mixture.'

'Harold, this is some sort of record. Are you sure–?'

'She can't deny any of them, she's signed that confession.'

'That doesn't mean anything–' Joe took another tack: 'Harold, when you are away on these sea trips, do you – you know what I mean? Get dirty water off your chest?'

'You mean with prostitutes? No, I don't!' Pincole looked offended, as if paying for sex was an abuse of charity. 'Once in a while, with a passenger–'

'You carry passengers on your ship?'

'Only six – people who aren't in a hurry to get anywhere. Sometimes the sea air and that, boredom, things like that, it gets to a woman travelling alone–'

'And it gets to you, too? If Eloise – that her true name?' Pincole nodded. 'What about her?'

'That's different. I don't think of myself being, well, like unfaithful to her–'

Here we go again, thought Joe: the double standard. He often wondered who had been the first to set the standard; he must trace the history of it. He changed tack again: 'I

65

don't want to get too personal, but – when you're with Eloise, how is it? Is she cool towards you?'

'Hell, no! We're never out of bed–'

Joe looked at the confession he held, then back at Pincole. 'How do I put this delicately? Is she – is she a nymphomaniac?'

Pincole pondered this for a moment, as if he had been asked if Eloise was a hypochondriac or a kleptomaniac. Then: 'I guess she might be. I'd never thought about it, till I found out about these fifteen guys.'

'Well, I don't think we should bring up the subject. It's just between me, you and – and Eloise.' He had trouble with the name.

When Harold Pincole had gone Joe went out to his outer office. He employed two secretaries, who he used as sounding boards. 'Well, what did you think of Mr Pincole's case?'

Edith Barker was in her fifties, plump and comfortable with her job; one doubted that she would ever need any legal advice. 'He should've stayed at home.'

'What's his wife like?' Shanyne Smith was twenty-eight going on eighteen, but she was a wizard on the office computer and Joe would not have swapped her for a sexpot with a 160 IQ.

'Is she a looker? She must be. Fifteen guys! Even Paris Hilton hasn't had that many.'

'Who's Paris Hilton?' asked Joe, who never read gossip magazines. 'I've never met Eloise–'

'Eloise?' echoed Edith.

'I know. Eloise the nymphomaniac – I'm going to have trouble keeping a straight face... Well, I'm going out. You can get me on my mobile if any more of her lovers turn up. I'll be with my sister-in-law, advising her on how to screw publishers for bigger royalties.'

'I'm looking forward to reading her book,' said Edith.

'There's a copy on my desk–'

2

He went out to his car, bending against the strength of the wind. Rain, which was desperately needed, was predicted. There were times, after the divorce, when he had had the mad idea to uproot his practice and take it to a country town. But there was too much heartache out there, with the drought; and no comedy. He got into his car and sat thinking for almost five minutes while the wind clawed at the wound-up windows and threw a spittle of rain across the windscreen. He was going to advise Marie how and where to invest the money, but he knew that Leif would have other plans for it. Marriage could be wrecked on many rocks; he knew that from experience. He just hoped that *Barney's Bank Job* would not be a hidden reef.

He looked back at the big house. His office was in a large old-time mansion; he lived in a flat above it. He had bought the house with three others: an accountant, an actuary and a doctor: health, death and taxes available at going rates. It had been his one and only investment, and it had proved to be a mid-Victorian goldmine, with buttresses and ornate balconies. It was situated, along with other mansions, Victorian, Edwardian and modern, in Strathfield, an area which did not think of itself as *suburban* but as an enclave surrounded by suburbs. It had once been a nest of solicitors, some of them living in the mansions, but now it had *suburbia* nibbling at its edges. There were several good private schools in the area, plus a school for the performing arts, like a chorus girl amongst nuns. The scent of the area, from its many trees, was that of gentility. A certain raffish element had crept in over the past few years, but they, perhaps unknowingly, were being converted.

Joe drove out through the iron gates of the large garden that fronted the mansion. He knew back streets that kept him off the clogged main road to the city, an artery suffering from traffic cholesterol. He drove with controlled exhilaration and so far had managed to avoid the birdshit of speeding tickets. He went through the city, crossed the Harbour Bridge and soon was in Wollstonecraft, another country.

Marie was opening the front door as he was opening the front gate. If she got to heaven before the rest of them she would open the Pearly Gates and tell St Peter to find something else to do. She was not an organizer, just toey.

She gave him a hug and a warm kiss. 'That should make the neighbours gossip. You should've brought champagne and flowers.'

'They're in the car. Can we go in before the neighbours start taking pictures? How are things?'

She led him through to the kitchen where coffee and cake waited; he was *family*. 'It's store-bought cake–'

'Love, I live alone. Everything I eat is

store-bought.'

He had met Marie when he was two years out at university and working for a top legal firm. He still played cricket for the university and he met her at a cricket barbecue. He had taken her out a couple of times, kissed her goodnight, but it came to nothing. Then she had introduced him to Louise and from then on he had been wrapped, and rapt, in the Micklethwaite twins.

'What's worrying you, Mar? You're more jumpy than usual.'

'Is it that apparent?' She poured coffee; not *instant*. Her mother had railed against instant coffee, teabags and sliced bread; Norah had lived in a past already long gone and never retrievable. 'I dunno, Joe. I'm just – not bewildered, but I'm still struggling to take it all in. My publishers rang this morning – there are two more foreign offers. Why would Hungarian kids be interested in a story about Australian kids?'

'Kids are more alike than adults–'

'It's all just piling up–'

'Good.' He bit into the coconut cake, the sort his mother used to make but not as good. 'I think you'd better let me handle the investment of all the lucre that's rolling in.'

She looked at him shrewdly. 'You don't

trust Leif to handle it?'

He was not surprised at the question. 'Do you? Come on, Mar. I'm not criticizing Leif – well, no, I guess I am. But what does he know about handling investments?'

She nodded, as if suddenly deciding she did not have to defend Leif. 'Nothing. He's in government – as he says, what does a government know about investment? It only knows how to take in money, not how to make it grow.'

Joe, too, nodded. Lately, like so many others, he had become disillusioned about politics. 'Too true. So what does he suggest you do with all this money? Assuming, of course, that promises become solid cash.'

'You think I'm counting my chickens too soon?'

'Love, in my game you wouldn't believe the number of chickens that don't get hatched.'

She nodded again. 'Leif wants to spend it. He's like some dizzy blonde – well, he *is* blond, isn't he? We're arguing about it–'

Joe did some sums on his notepad, then snapped it shut. 'Okay, I'll talk to your publishers and we'll get a new contract drawn up. You did the wise thing not signing it. We won't screw them for a big advance–'

He shook his head again. 'The book's been

out – what? Two weeks? I'll get the royalty percentage as high as I can. And nothing for them out of the TV deal.'

'I think you'd screw the St Vincent de Paul–' But she looked at him admiringly, and with affection bordering on love. *Why did Louise ever let him go?* 'You're my man, Joe–'

'Number 2 man,' he said 'How are the kids?'

'Fine. We're taking them up to see Dad at the weekend. We'll spend a coupla days up there in one of the cottages the retirement village owns.'

He kissed her on the cheek, squeezed her arm and left. There was not much of the afternoon left, so he decided against going back to the office. He drove into the city, parked his car in a parking station, and walked along to Dampiers. He did not like the narrow streets of the city, the tall buildings rearing above him, the feeling of being hemmed in. He was not a man of the wide-open spaces, but at least in the suburbs one could breathe. It was one of the reasons he had left the major law firm five years ago and moved out to Strathfield. A minor odyssey, not to be compared to that of Hume and Hovell, but a satisfactory one.

Not at all sure why, he was on his way to see Louise. She was at the Chapelli counter, doing no business: rich customers did not come into the store this late in the afternoon. She smiled brightly at him, glad that he had appeared, though her raised eyebrow said she was puzzled why he was here.

'Buying for yourself or for some lady friend?'

'Quit the wisecracks.' He still used words that had gone out of fashion years ago, as if knee-deep in a rubbish tip of colloquialisms. 'I just wanted to see you.'

'Joe—' There were moments when her love for him was as strong as it had once been. They came like flashes of recognition of memory that was too often, almost deliberately, faint. 'Where have you been? In court?'

'No. Seeing Marie. Can you knock off early and I'll take you for a drink?'

She looked at her watch; not a Chapelli bauble. 'It's almost time. Give me ten minutes, I'll meet you at the main entrance. You look very distinguished.'

'A new suit. The girls in the office told me I was starting to look like I always dressed in the dark. I was wearing it the other night, but you didn't notice.'

He had once remarked that fashion was

73

for sheep who liked conmen for their shepherds. Louise, who knew what made the world go round, had told him to wash his mouth out.

When she came out of the store just before closing time he felt the pride he had always felt: not in *owning* her, but just in being with her. He knew the difference in pride between that of a man, and that of a woman. Women did, but rarely, take pride in possession. That was one thing he had learned in divorce cases, which had taught him more about human nature than university had.

He took her to the Sheraton-on-the-Park and they sat in the lounge and looked at each other across their drinks: a light beer for him, vodka-and-tonic for her. Their only common taste in drinks had run to wine. 'I've spent a couple of hours with Marie. Our girl isn't as happy as she might be.'

'She seemed happy enough at the launch–'

'She's now counting the pennies. Or rather, Leif is and he wants to spend them. He's a bugger for living for the moment.'

'There are a lot like that. Marie used to be like it.'

'Things have changed, at least with her. She suddenly sees this big wave looming over her, all money, and it's, I dunno, it's scared her.

Do you have any influence with Leif? I can't lean on him, I'm just his brother-in-law–'

'I can try, but how do I bring it up? I can't just barge in there–'

He sipped his beer, then nodded. 'No, you're right. I think Marie is a bit bewildered by it all. How would you handle it if you were suddenly in the money?'

'I was reading about that woman Rowling and the Harry Potter books – she's earned *millions*. How would you handle it? You're worth more than Marie is going to be.'

He grinned. 'You been checking on me? I don't let it go to my head. So you've got no suggestion how we rein in Leif?'

'I'll give it some thought. But sisters shouldn't interfere in each other's marriages.'

He grinned again, in good humour at being with her. 'You should come out some time to my office and see how I have to interfere.' He finished his beer, put down his glass. Though she didn't notice it, it was a deliberate motion, as if he had been working towards it for the last half-hour. Which he had: 'You want to have dinner?'

She recognized the moment, but something held her back. She finished her drink, put the glass carefully back on the table. 'Not tonight, Joe. I'm worn out – really.

Some other time?'

'Sure,' he said and managed to keep the disappointment out of his voice. 'And give some thought to Marie and Leif. And their kids. There's something wrong with things when good fortune becomes a burden.'

'You're wise,' she said, loving him.

'Fat lotta good it does me. Come on, I'll get you a cab.'

They went out into the street, he raised a hand and, miraculously, a cab slid into the kerb. He kissed her cheek, put her into the cab, gave the driver some money and Louise's address, then stood back as the cab slid away.

He looked after it, his heart full, even if hurting.

Chapter Four

1

Leif never thought of himself as selfish or traitorous; temptation was always temporary. He loved Marie, his only love; all the others were just diversions. Dinah Camplin had come gift-wrapped, by herself, and he hadn't been able to resist the temptation.

He worked as the principal public relations man and minder for a lesser government department, the Ministry for Intra-Urban Development, a brief that no one seemed able to understand. It had been a bright idea at the time by the Premier, a man given to bright ideas that, like faulty globes, too often went on the blink. The ministry had gradually sunk into the back-end of Cabinet, like the last flag on the tail-end of a kite. It still had the same minister as at its beginning. He was an ex-union official of the Brotherhood of Truckies and had come to the post with an open mind, which meant, in effect, he hadn't a clue what it was about. But he had learned, coached by Leif, that in all government ministries, if the paper flowed, the stream never stopped running. Reports were commissioned annually, each one being tabled as the next year's was started. Leif, as much as anyone, kept everything going and everyone in work. No government, in election year, demolishes a ministry and throws two thousand workers out on the street. Unless, of course, the cost and wastage became public...

Leif had occasionally seen Dinah, cleavage at the ready like a free lucky dip, on his floor at the ministry, but he knew she came from another section. She would flash him a smile, like a welcoming semaphore, but he had given her no more than a smile in return. He did his best, even though it was poor, to keep temptation out of the office. His minister was a newly-born Christian and had even suggested, but to deaf ears, that there should be a prayer breakfast once a week. Any liaisons in the office were to be frowned upon. The heathens took notice and even mild flirtation took a cooling bath.

Then there was a small reception in one of the big rooms at Parliament House and Dinah was there, cleavage reduced to a wink. Marie occasionally attended these receptions and enjoyed them, but she had begged off this evening, saying it was not worth the cost of a babysitter. *Barney's Bank Job* was about to be pushed by her publishers and the excitement still had to come. She was not counting pennies, but kept a tight hand on dollars.

So Leif, half an hour into a dreary reception, handing out platitudes to the media freeloaders along with the canapés and drinks, had found himself beside Dinah.

'Bored?'

'You must be, buttering-up everyone–' Her voice was her only drawback; it seemed to be high in her palate. She wore a dark blue dress, buttoned at the neck but with an opening below the button that hinted at the hidden goods. She wasn't too obvious, but she was anybody's dinner or drinks date for the evening. Leif should have been cautious, but he *was* bored and boredom clouds the vision. 'But you're good at it. I mean that as a compliment.'

'It comes with the job.' And the pay was good. Not as high as some other minders got, but he was happy with it. He knew that if he got twice as much as his current salary, he would spend it all. Money, as he would tell Marie, was meant to be spent. 'You're in

Complaints. That must be worse.'

'Not really. Most of the complaints are from developers and they were born to complain. Can I buy you a drink – somewhere else?' She was as blatant as a political smile.

He hesitated, but only for a moment. 'Sure, why not? Better leave separately – we don't want people talking.'

'Do you care?'

'Yes,' he said and felt something like a stab of conscience. But it didn't stake him to the floor and after a minute or two he left.

Out in Macquarie Street, with the stern Georgian façade of Parliament House behind them, she looked at him. 'Would you like to see me home? I'm not a very good cook, but I have a gourmet microwave.'

He hesitated, looked at his watch. He usually did not get home from receptions like tonight's before 10 or 10.30: it was now only 5 past 8. Temptation is often timed by the clock. 'Where do you live?'

'South Coogee–' That was a relief; he was afraid she might live at Palm Beach or to the south, at Como. 'I have my own flat–'

'My car's in the MPs' garage. Come on–'

She lived in a small flat on the ground floor of a block of four that dated from the 1930s and, accordingly, had thick walls, which he would come to appreciate. The flats were in a steep street looking west to Randwick cemetery. The graves ran in neat rows up a slope, like a stone audience waiting for the show to begin, a show that was already over. It lent a rather sombre air to what went on in the houses and flats across from it and Leif wondered if the bedroom curtains were always drawn. Dinah's flat was better than he had expected, more than comfortably furnished. He put aside the thought that she might earn a bit on the side or any other position; she was libidinous but not commercial. Or he hoped not...

She must have read his mind, because she said, 'I'm a country girl and my mother insists I live comfortably. They have a property, wool and beef, out the back of Merriwa.'

'Is the drought hitting them?' It was fencing talk while they waited to see who would undo the first button.

'They're doing it tough–' She undid the button that held her dress at her throat. 'Do you want to eat?'

'No,' he said and took her in his arms; or rather, she took him.

He began to undress her; or, being an Irish Protestant, to disrobe her. Nude, she was startling, even despite the hints she gave when dressed; she was, as he thought of it, *endowed*. They went to bed, her technique proving as wide as his. They were bedmates, if not soulmates.

When at last he got out of bed, as exhausted as if he had been in a Baghdad trench, he sat for a moment, his back to her. He was always like this after every dalliance (another of his favourite words): trying to clear his mind of what had gone on before he went home. Conscience did not make him giddy, but it did, for a moment or two, make him light-headed. He looked over his shoulder at her.

'You mind if I have a shower?'

'You want to wash me off you?' If she was offended, she didn't show it. She sounded more amused, as if used to it.

Yes; but he didn't say it. 'No, I've had a long day. I want to wake myself up to drive home–'

'Go ahead.' She drew the sheet up to cover herself; the curtain was down, the show was over. 'I think you and I are matched.'

'How do you mean?' He turned right round to face her. 'Do you have a husband or a boyfriend?'

'I had a *partner*–' She underlined the word. She was sitting up in bed, the sheet drawn up above her breasts, as if modesty had suddenly occurred to her, like a chill. 'He was so damned *possessive*–'

'And you don't like being possessed?'

'No. I'm – what do they call it? – a free soul.'

He doubted if she had a soul, but now was not the time for religious debate. 'I'll have my shower–'

He was in the shower when she opened the shower door. But he held up a hand; he wanted to get home before temptation held him there for the rest of the night. 'Men only–'

She smiled, like a cat that had not only won Best in Show, but the winner's cup was full of milk. 'There'll be other times–'

That had been six weeks ago and he had been to her flat three times since then. She showed no hint that she wanted to possess him, but she always made herself available. Adultery is a state of mind; it is doubtful if it ever concerned Casanova or other famous rakes. But he always had bouts of penance that had him taking home gifts for Marie and Brigid and Rosie. They were still the buoys that kept him afloat.

Then came Marie's success and the night of the book's launch. Dinah came to him the day before and offered her services as a babysitter. He wanted to laugh at the thought and his first reaction was to say No. But she persisted.

'Look, I'm not going to play worm in the apple. I'm *interested* in you – not just the sex. I've seen those two little girls of yours – your wife brought them to the office one day – they look absolute angels–'

'They're not that–'

He should not have kept talking; in the end he agreed to her babysitting for the night. And it had all passed off smoothly, with the kids and Marie liking her. And she liking them. He would have to be careful or he would have a *ménage-à-cinque.*

At the office they kept well apart; if she had to come to his floor it was 'Mr Johnson' and 'Ms Camplin'. The distance between them was discreet; like a cardinal and a nun, though the simile did not occur to him, a non-religious man. If any of his staff suspected any liaison it did not show. Alone together, always at her flat, the sex was as exciting as it had been the first night: neither took the other for granted. He called her *honey* in bed, a term he had never used before, and she called him *lover*. In his more sober, less aroused moments he shook his head at the endearments. He made one mistake and called Marie *honey* and he made sure it did not occur again.

But he was walking a tightrope that threatened at any moment to slip from beneath his feet and hit him in the crotch.

Chapter Five

1

One Saturday morning, the weather, though midwinter, almost spring-like, Louise and Marie, accompanied by Leif and the two girls, drove up to Bide-a-While, the retirement village where Matt Micklethwaite lived. The name of the place always brought on a bilious attack for Matt. 'Did you ever hear such crap? I put a bag over my head before I tell anyone where I live.'

'Dad, the developers have trouble finding names for the number of retirement places going up. There are more Oases, Springs, Havens than you'd find in an atlas.' But Louise had got little thanks for her remark.

Marie and Brigid and Rosie were to stay Saturday night at one of the three cottages that the retirement village kept for visitors. The whole village fronted onto a small beach, one of those on this Central Coast strip. It was ideal for children, no big surf, and, so far, no sharks, except, as Matt said, for the developers buying up the remaining shoreline.

Leif and the girls were down on the beach and Louise and Marie were sitting with their father in the shade of a low-branched pine. Matt was in his late sixties; he had skin like bark and a body of hardwood. Except for the arthritis, which could occasionally cripple him. He had been a master plumber, with extensive work on the North Shore, and he had looked after his money – 'Don't ask me if I made a comfortable living. Cleaning out blocked toilets, crawling under houses over ant-beds, getting soaked through from a burst pipe – I made an *un*comfortable living–'

'Stop moaning, Dad–' It was a family hymn, sung without malice.

Now Louise was saying, 'How are you getting on with Dr Teddes?'

He was the retirement village's visiting doctor 'He's older'n I am, he's bloody useless. Suggests a good night's sleep should cure insomnia. If you're light-headed, he prescribes farting–'

'Dad, you're the bloody end!' said Marie. 'I dunno why one of your clients didn't clock you with a piece of pipe!'

He had a pleasant smile and knew how to

use it. 'What's the point of being old if you can't complain?... Here come the kids!'

They came up from the beach, wet and freckled with sand, and flung themselves on him. Louise, quiet and observant, remembered her father's and her mother's disappointment when she had had the miscarriage. And suddenly felt motherly and took Rosie on her lap.

'I'm all wet and sandy–'

'It doesn't matter, darling. These are just some old rags I threw on–' Her slacks were by Prada and her shirt by Gant, bought at a sale, but she felt reckless, maternal. 'Do you like the water?'

'Fantastic! I think I'd like to be a shark.'

'We'll work on it, darling. Lady sharks don't have too good a time of it–'

Beside them, with Brigid on his knee, Matt was querying Marie on her turn of events: 'How's it feel, being rich and famous?'

'Stop exaggerating. I'm neither rich nor famous. I'm still trying to take it all in–'

Leif, with his arm round her, said, 'She's handling it well, Matt. A little tight with the money, but it's not going to her head. Just into the bank.'

'A good place for it to be,' said Matt, who had long ago recognized his son-in-law's

88

profligacy. 'For the time being... Take it easy, Marie, whatever happens. I saw some of my North Shore customers, when the IT boom went to their heads. One month, up there on cloud nine, the next they couldn't pay their bills. My motto has always been never hurry, never worry.'

'You just hurried us, worried us,' said Marie, who had always loved him but been his severest critic. 'Mum sometimes wanted to shoot you, but she didn't know how to load a gun.'

He smiled again. 'I'm surprised you didn't show her how. Has she ever threatened to shoot you, Leif?'

'Just once or twice,' said Leif and squeezed Marie's shoulder. 'I just go out and mow the lawn till she gets over it. Or wash the car.'

'You can't do that these days, with all the water restrictions. I'd be making a mint, fitting economy heads to showers and taps.'

'And abusing the customers,' said Marie.

Louise had always liked the company of her father. She was not his favourite, he didn't play favourites, but she had always felt that she understood him better than her mother or Marie. She knew he had had his dreams, though he was never specific about them. And she knew the hole in his life that had occurred when Norah had died. She leaned across and pressed his hand now and he smiled at her, as if some secret message had passed between them.

Then he looked at Brigid. 'What'll we do while you're up here? You want to go to McDonald's?'

'Fantastic!' said Brigid and Rosie.

'You'll get fat—'

Both girls wrinkled their noses, as if getting fat was no hazard at all.

Louise looked at Leif, each holding one of the girls, and he winked at her. She had no idea what the wink implied or invited, but suddenly she was seeing him as nobody's husband, nobody's father, just a blond hulk in shorts and a V-neck cotton sweater. Under Rosie's bum she felt a stirring in her crotch. She knew, suddenly, what loomed ahead, once she and Leif were in his car on the way back to Sydney. She slid Rosie off her lap, as if divesting conscience.

Leif kissed Marie's cheek, stood up. 'Time we were getting back.'

'How's the government?' asked Matt. He had been a Labor voter, but had become disillusioned and now thought politics was a playground where the voters were kept out. Most of his fellow residents were Liberal voters, but he never got into arguments with them, though he could be argumentative. 'Still looking every which way but the right way? I read that they actually had a train that ran on time last week – all the passengers fainted and had to be carried off. You're a useless lotta bastards.'

'You're always swearing, Pa,' said Brigid.

'Keeps me young,' said her grandfather and kissed her and her sister.

Louise kissed him, gave him a hug, then hugged Marie. Almost like an act of contrition in advance. 'I'll feed him and keep an eye on him.'

'He needs a rest,' said Marie. 'He's worried about his arthritis getting worse.'

We're talking about the wrong man. 'Dad'll weather it. As he said, what's the point of getting old if you can't complain? Right, Dad?'

He smiled at both of them. He was a loving father, an old-fashioned sort who could only show his affection for them by hugging and kissing his grandchildren.

Leif shook hands with him. 'I have to work tomorrow – the boss is guest speaker at his old union's annual meeting. The Brotherhood of Truckies.'

'Brotherhood? We're getting more bloody

91

American by the day.'

'Time you went,' said Marie to Leif. 'He's getting grumpy again.' She kissed him again. 'Drive carefully. Look after Lou.'

Matt was still grumpy: 'Brotherhood!'

'You better get used to it, buddy,' said Leif, grinning. 'It's the way of the world now. Listen up.'

'Listen *up?* Whoever listens *down?* Holy Christ!'

'You're swearing again, Pa,' said Brigid.

'No, I'm not, love. I'm just praying for the English language.'

'Okey-doke,' said Brigid and her grandfather gave up.

The Johnsons had come up the coast in two cars, Marie bringing Louise in the Corolla and Leif with the two girls in the Volvo. Marie was to keep the Corolla for her return tomorrow and Leif was taking Louise home in the Volvo. Two-car families experience problems that one-car families wish they had.

Leif drove fast, but with care, enjoying the experience. Louise, a relaxed passenger, even (as Joe once remarked) in a runaway truck, sat beside him, doing nothing to throw cold water on the feeling inside her. They were crossing the Hawkesbury River

Bridge, beginning the long climb up the slope south of it, when she said, 'You want to come home for a meal?'

He looked sideways at her, hardly moving his head. 'Do you want to go to the trouble? We can have a bite somewhere.'

For a moment conscience opened a gate; but she closed it. 'No, I've got leftovers from last night. Some beef burgundy and half a peach pie.' She was a good cook and enjoyed it. It wasn't ambrosia or whatever it was that houris served. But then he was no caliph, though he did have a faint resemblance to a god, one with clay feet but great thighs.

'You go to all that trouble for yourself?'

'I enjoy it.' And it fills in empty time.

They were fencing and both knew it. The late afternoon rushed at them through the windscreen. 'Sure, okay. Beef burgundy–' He exaggeratedly licked his lips, smiled at her. Lasciviously? She hoped so.

They were close to her home when he said, 'Where's there a bottle shop? We'll stop and get a good bottle of red.'

'There's no need, I've got some,' she said, everything managed.

As they went up the stairs to her flat, her next-door neighbours, the Frazers, came out of their flat. She introduced them; then: 'My brother-in-law. He's brought me – we've been up to see my father–'

Shut up, Louise. She was gabbling, like a schoolgirl trying smuggle in the school lecher.

The Frazers smiled and went on down the stairs. Louise was sure that they were nodding knowingly to each other. She looked at Leif: 'A single woman has to be careful. Gossip–'

'Of course,' said Leif and he, too, smiled knowingly.

Before they ate they sat out on her small balcony and looked at the water while they sipped their drinks. Out on the bay a low-slung craft, perhaps a scow, glided silently and darkly towards the far shore. The sky was flat, high cirrus cloud serrated by the setting sun; even as they watched, the serrations turned blood-red and the sky looked like a cracked ceiling on fire.

'I love sunsets,' she said.

'I prefer mornings.' She knew he went jogging most mornings. 'I wish we had a water view.'

'Maybe you can move, if things come good for Marie.'

Why do we have to mention her? It was idle

talk, still fencing, but conscience kept coming in, like an unwelcome swordsman. They went in to dinner, warmed up in the microwave and somehow not spoiled. The wine was good, a shiraz that, she now remembered, had been a present from Joe. Why was she being pricked from all angles because of what she had in mind?

'You know how to choose a wine,' said Leif, savouring it. 'It's a beaut.'

Shut up and finish it.

They did the washing-up, like husband and wife; then he dropped the tea-towel and took her in his arms. He said nothing, and kissed her as if it had been agreed all along that that was what was to be done. As it had been.

They went into the bedroom and she took her clothes off as naturally as she did every night. She got into bed, saying nothing, watching him as he stripped, aware that everything she had expected was there and the proper size. He climbed in beside her, looked at her for a moment as if expecting her to change her mind. Then he went to work.

And that was what it was: work. Or an exercise. When it was all over he lay beside her exhausted, as if waiting to fall into a quick sleep before repeating the exercise. And she lay beside him, feeling she had been in a steeplechase in which she was the hurdles. She was empty of all but a terrible shame and anger at herself. She remembered something, like an empty bar of music, from Shakespeare, whom she had read in her one year of Arts at university. *He will not manage her, though he mount her.* The reverse was true. There was no way in the world she meant anything to him other than another cheap lay.

She lay with her eyes closed for a minute or two while she took in – what? She was not sure; it was not disappointment, she had not built any hopes on a relationship. And, if she told herself the truth, had not wanted one; she could not have gone on betraying Marie. It had been, now she considered it, no more than an act of discovery. And she had foundered on the sea of his indifference. She wondered if other women had been disappointed in him, but abruptly put the thought out of her mind. That way might lead to Marie and wondering what *she* had found, if anything.

He stroked her shoulder. 'Good?'

'Good enough.'

She got out of bed, went into the bathroom and took a shower. She stood under it for ten minutes; to hell with water restrictions. It was as if she wanted the water to wash everything out of her: disappointment, shame, conscience. At last she got out, dried herself, looked at herself in the big mirror. There was no apparent change from the way she had looked this morning. She wrapped the towel round herself, covering everything from the top of her breasts to her crotch, then went back into the bedroom.

He was sitting up in bed, leaning against the pillows, ready for more exercise. 'How was that?' She didn't answer, then he looked at her and saw the change in her. 'That's it? No more?'

'That's it.' She sat down on the side of the bed, away from him. 'That's it,' she repeated. *Please don't be dumb, Leif, and make me spell it out.* 'It would never work.'

'What wouldn't work?'

He was deliberately being dumb. 'Leif–' As if spelling it out to a child: 'I don't want to get into a triangle with Marie–'

'Leave her out of it!' He was suddenly angry.

'We can't leave her out of it–' How could he be so blind or dumb or whatever? 'I should never have got into this in the first place–'

'Why did you?'

Wait a minute – why is he interrogating me?
'I honestly don't know. Maybe it was just horniness – we suffer from it like you men. I just don't know, Leif. But I'm sorry now and it's not going to happen again.'

'Jesus!' He shook his head, as if he had never been rebuffed before. She wondered how women felt when they were rebuffed; then put the thought out of her head. *Don't go into deeper waters, Louise.*

'You'd better have a shower and get dressed.' As if still talking to a child. She was not going to drop the towel and start dressing in front of him. Modesty had suddenly become a defence. 'It's over, Leif. Get used to it.'

She took a dressing-gown from the closet, went out into the living room and put it on, slipping off the towel. She was composed now, a little to her surprise; though she had always been the less excitable of herself and Marie. But Marie kept cropping up in her mind and guilt was slowly creeping through her like a virus. Conscience, she was learning, can sometimes be as heavy an affliction as elephantiasis.

He must have hurried his shower, because in less than ten minutes he came into the living room dressed in his shorts and top, his hair still wet and combed back straight, no fancy coiffure. To have it standing up straight on his head, arrayed disarray, as if he had been affronted, would only have made her laugh. The shower must have cleared his brain, because he was less argumentative, less hard done by. He wasn't smiling, but he wasn't glowering.

'How do we handle this from now on?' His tone was almost plaintive and, against her will, she found herself liking him for it. The eyes, she had read, were the mirror of the soul. Balls. Voices were the direct link, forget about mirrors.

'Just as before, Leif. We tried something, it didn't work. It's behind us,' she said and drew the robe more tightly round herself.

From somewhere he dredged up a smile, weak but genuine. 'You win.'

She didn't think so, but she wasn't going to be magnanimous. She just nodded and he nodded back. Then, without a further word, he turned and left; she hoped he would not meet the Frazers on the stairs. She was surprised, and relieved, that he left no empty space behind him.

She went into the bedroom, stripped the sheets and remade the bed. Then she put on a nightgown, got into bed, stared at the ceiling for almost five minutes, then turned out the light.

Out on the bay a pleasure boat went by, music playing: Delta Goodrem was singing 'Innocent Eyes'. The irony, Louise thought as she fell asleep, was too obvious.

2

Sunday morning she got up, dressed casually and went to Mass in a neighbouring parish. She wanted to be amongst strangers, not be recognized and welcomed. It was not an act of contrition, nor an act of communion. It was trying to get her thoughts straight, a search for a calm new sea. She had no thoughts of becoming a regular churchgoer, a sinner coming back to the fold; the Church would have to change a lot before that happened. She sat in the half-filled church, at the back of a congregation made up mostly of greyheads and baldheads, and listened to an old priest give an old sermon. But, somehow, a peace of sorts settled on her.

She went back to the flat, got into shorts and sat out on her balcony in the hard-to-believe winter sun. She read the weekend newspapers, one of her pleasures. The bad news was no worse than last week's; the good news was that there was *some* good news. She made herself a sandwich, then fell asleep as the sun crept slowly westwards. Then at 4 o'clock she was woken by the phone: it was Joe.

'Are you clothed or naked?'

'Stark naked. I'm out on the balcony and there are eighteen men out on the bay with their glasses on me'

'Can I come over? Dressed or undressed. I want to talk to you.'

'There's nothing in the house. Bring something and I'll feed you.'

An hour later he arrived. As she opened the door to him, the Frazers came out of the neighbouring door. Smiling inwardly, she introduced Joe: 'My lawyer.'

They said hello to Joe, then went on down the stairs smiling to each other. They had moved in only a fortnight before and she was sure they had now marked her as a loose woman.

'I'm your lawyer?' Joe said as she closed the front door behind him.

'Ex-husbands have to be explained. What have you brought?'

He had brought pizza, salad mix, tomatoes, ice-cream and a tin of blueberries, his long-time favourite. 'I forgot the wine. But you should have a bottle – I brought one last time.'

The one she had shared with Leif last night. 'I'm saving that. There's a bottle of white in the fridge, a semillon, I think.'

'I'm a chardonnay-quaffing leftie, m'self.'

It was approach talk, the same as she had had with Leif last night. But this evening was not going to be a repeat of last night. *No way, Jose.*

Half an hour later Joe got down to brass tacks; or golden tacks. 'We're going to worry about Marie–'

'We?'

'You and me. You're her twin sister, I'm her loving brother-in-law.'

'What about her loving husband?' She wished she could get Leif out of her mind.

'He loves her, but he's bloody useless. Our girl stands a good chance of being disappointed–'

'But she's got all those wonderful contracts!'

'Not yet. I've seen the offers and on paper they're great. But so far she hasn't had anything to sign. If everything goes as they promise, she'll make a million, maybe two. Not big money by some standards – some top

CEOs make that every year as salary. But it'll make her a rich housewife, or anyway not a desperate one.'

'So what's her problem? She wiped the last of the pizza from her mouth.

'I've been doing a bit of reading–' He had always been a researcher. It had been a joke between them that he wouldn't open a toilet roll till he'd read the instructions on the packaging. 'There was an English woman writer got an advance of half a million quid. At the end of six months she had sold only 18,000 copies. She owes them around 475 thousand quid.'

'Does she have to pay it back?'

'No, but I'll bet her next book she'll get a ten-bob advance. We have to protect Marie against any possible disappointment.'

'What if she makes five or six million and it goes to her head?'

'Do you think it would?'

'No-o. But I dunno...'

'Dan Brown, the guy who wrote *The Da Vinci Code*, he got something like a 50,000-dollar advance. Christ knows what he's made since. But from what I've read, he's still got his feet on the ground. Marie will keep her feet on the ground, but we may have to hold down Leif.'

'I should kick you out of here. I think you're in love with my sister.'

'Don't be nasty, Lou–'

She had meant it as a joke, but now the echo was in her ears: she sounded jealous. 'I'm sorry – I didn't mean it that way–'

He had been about to sip his wine, but now he lowered the glass and looked at her. 'What's the matter, Lou?'

She hesitated before answering, not wanting to give anything away. 'I don't know, Joe. It's not jealousy of Marie – I'm thrilled for her. And the kids. And even Leif. It's none of that... My life, my own life, just seems to be aimless.'

To her relief he didn't move to sit beside her. 'Lou, half the bloody world goes round in circles. The other half goes the other way.'

'You're no help – you're a pessimist–'

'No, a realist.'

She pulled herself together; inwardly, so that he wouldn't notice. 'What are we to do for Marie, then?'

'I want you to work on Leif – you're closer to him than I am, he's your brother-in-law–'

Oh great! 'You're more practical than I am – you know money better than I do–'

'It's not the money – well, it is, but it's only part of the problem. I don't think Marie

104

knows how big it may be – the problem, I mean. Leif certainly doesn't. She may go on to write another bestseller, one never knows. But by then she will know the problems–'

'You talk as if being a success is a problem in itself.'

'It is for a lot of people. Look at the number of pop and rock singers who can't handle it. Marie is not going to be like that. But Leif could be. He won't envy Marie her success, if it comes – he's not a bastard–'

He is, you know. Just as I'm a bitch.

'–but he'll go the wrong way about helping her enjoy it. I spent two hours with her last week and she told me more than she thought she did.'

'You bloody sneaky lawyers–'

He grinned. 'That's why she employed me. More wine?'

She looked at him, affectionately. 'You're still part of us, aren't you?'

He took his time before nodding. 'You and I buggered up things, but–' He didn't finish, just drank the last of his wine and stood up. 'Time I was going–'

He lifted her hand and kissed it. He often did it, without flourish or embarrassment for the woman whose hand he put close to his lips. It had started as a gag, but now he did it without mocking it.

'Do Spanish men still do that, kiss a woman's hand?'

'I dunno. My dad, even though he was a socialist, did it. Still does, sometimes. My mum came from a family that had been aristocrats back in, I think, the seventeenth century. The blue blood was pretty pale by the time it got to my mum, but she liked certain old-fashioned gestures. And Dad gave 'em to her. There's something about a gallant socialist, though you might have some trouble explaining that to some of the old-time Labor blokes.'

'Always be gallant,' she said and kissed him on the cheek, loving him. For the moment.

Chapter Six

1

The International Brotherhood of Truckers (Australian version: Truckies) was holding its annual international convention in Sydney for the first time. The Ministry of Tourism had promised everything at a discount: hotels, restaurants, casino, brothels, all necessary conveniences for a convention of robust men and a few less robust and less brothel-inclined women delegates. The Minister for Intra-Urban Development, being a Truckies union man, was guest speaker on this Sunday, greetings day.

The Minister was short, thin and wispy, an unlikely truckie, unless it was on a fork-lift. He had a deep, surprisingly strong voice, developed over the years at union meetings where a soft voice got no votes. He had been a seven-days-a-week sinner in his younger days, but two years ago he had become a born-again Christian and, like all converts to anything, worked harder at salvation, his own and others', than those born to their faith. Heaven, Joe Fernandez, an agnostic, once said, will be hell when the converts take over.

The minister was a decent man and Leif liked him and got on well with him His first name was Cyril, but anyone who called him that was dead; he was Steve Perkins to everyone, including his wife, who occasionally called him other names, much worse than Cyril. Leif wrote him good speeches and he delivered them with convincing fervour. Which couldn't be fervour from the truth, punned Opposition members in Parliament.

The American delegates to the convention were the best-dressed, most of them looking as if they owned a fleet of trucks. The local delegates wore their best suits, but smelled of mothballs; one looked for the blue singlet under the white shirts. The Russian and Chinese delegates looked almost as prosperous as the Americans, though *their* suits creaked with their newness. There were delegates from fifty-four countries, including a solitary delegate from Mauretania, a huge happy black man who had already applied to the Department of Immigration for permanent residence. It was, all in all, a happy gathering.

The get-together opening of the Brotherhood's convention was held in an exhibition hall at Darling Harbour. Minister Perkins made his speech, everyone cheered and clapped, which was the best way of getting rid of him quickly. Then the minister circulated while Leif stood on the sidelines and watched. Then it was over and the minister could leave.

'Can you drive me home, Leif? It's not out of your way, is it?' He lived in Sutherland, which was the South Pole to the North Pole of Wollstonecraft.

'Not at all,' said Leif, recognizing that the minister wanted to tell him something not on today's agenda. Steve Perkins loved his ministerial car, so something big and secret was probable if he had sacrificed the ride home in it.

Leif drove the Volvo sedately, not wanting to be startled when Steve gave him the good news. What would it be? Promotion of himself to another, larger ministry? Maybe even to the Premier's Department?

'Nice car,' said Perkins, who hadn't ridden in it before.

'I bought it last year, we're very happy with it.'

They rode in silence for a mile or two,

through flatlands that Leif only knew as an occasional visitor; he was sometimes surprised at how little he knew of his home city. Perkins, out of character, said nothing, as if this was unfamiliar territory for him too; he was not a man for silences, as if dangers lurked there. Then he said, the words almost bursting out of him, 'We've got a problem, Leif.'

Leif slowed the car a little, looked at Perkins. 'How's that? I thought everything's been going fine.'

'Better pull over, Leif.' Perkins looked uncomfortable, as if a police patrol car had been following them. 'We need to discuss this sitting still, not while you're driving.'

They were on a main road lined with used-car lots. Flags and banners shivered in the wind; blank messages were semaphored from hundreds of windscreens. Leif pulled into a No Parking zone, switched off the engine, pulled on the brake. Then he turned and faced Steve Perkins. 'What is it, Steve?'

Perkins looked out at the hundreds of cars, all guaranteed driven only by old ladies from home to store, then he looked back at Leif, took a deep breath and said, 'They're closing down the Ministry.'

'What!'

'We've been talking about it in Cabinet for the past week–'

'Jesus, *why?*'

'Treasury says we're not pulling our weight, never have. You know what he's like, Gerry Coker–'

The State Treasurer, a lugubrious man who was rumoured to be colour-blind: he saw red where everyone else saw black. 'Tightest-arsed bastard since Uriah Heep. But that's the only reason – saving money?'

Perkins nodded. 'The media have been at us – you know that.'

'The media are always more expert at anything than those of us who work at it... Jesus, Steve, government departments aren't supposed to save money. Coker's been spending too much time with the Top End of Town. It's okay for everyone else, from top to bottom, to fucking spend money, but we're supposed to count the fucking pennies!' Then, as if the two of them were isolated here in the front seat of the car, he said, 'What happens to you and me?'

'The ministry will be scaled down, it'll become the *Office* for Intra-Urban. The staff will be downsized, I dunno to what figure. And I'm afraid you'll be downgraded, you'll be on a lower salary–'

'Like hell I will! I'll fight 'em on that–'

'I'll back you, but it's going to be a tough fight–' For a moment Steve Perkins sounded like the union man he had once been.

'Jesus Christ, after all the fucking effort we put into it–'

'I wish you wouldn't keep invoking the Saviour–' The born-again Christian was offended.

'He's gunna be invoked a lot when the shit hits the hundred fans we'll be holding. Steve, can you imagine what it's going to be like when the union gets wind of this? How many will get the sack, be downsized, as they'll be told? Fifteen hundred, eighteen hundred–?'

Leif suddenly stopped talking, looked out of the car away from Steve Perkins. So this was where the world ended, here on a suburban main road flanked by hundreds of second-hand cars, empty shells with the setting sun reflected like a huge mockery on rows and rows of windscreens. He suddenly wanted to weep, something he hadn't done since he was a child.

'It was bound to come, Leif–' Perkins had never been a vain or ambitious man; he had been a fighter as a union man, but once in Parliament he had recognized his true worth and settled for whatever task he was given. He was a seat-warmer, but, to his credit, he actually worked. He would be demoted, but he wouldn't be sacked. 'You can go into the private sector, it's always looking for men who've worked in government–'

'I don't *want* to go into that–' There was a certain safety (or there had been) in government service. On the surface he looked an adventurer, Leif the Bold, but at heart he was a man who looked for comfort, for security.

'Well, you shouldn't have to worry too much. You'll be downgraded, but I gather your wife is gunna make a mint – my wife was telling me–' Perkins sometimes had the approach of a semi-trailer.

'I don't want to live off her!'

'Sorry–'

'Let's talk about it tomorrow. I'll take you home–'

But the car wouldn't start. He had run out of petrol. The end of the world was laughing at him.

2

Marie took the news as he expected: 'It's not

the end of the world.'

Oh, the slings and arrows of cliché! 'I'll be getting less money–'

'So? The mortgage will be out of the way with my money – we'll have some left over to invest. You won't have to work so hard–'

'Love, do you ever look on the dark side of things?'

She smiled at him, put a rubber-gloved hand against his cheek. 'Sweetheart, you have no idea...'

He had not told her the news last night, but had gone to bed brooding and hoping that, come Monday, it might prove to be no more than a half-baked idea, of which this government had proved to be master bakers. His natural optimism, his belief that the future would take care of itself, had struggled to surface, but when he fell asleep he was climbing a slippery slope. This morning the news, though not yet announced, had proved to be true: the ministry was finished. He had spent the morning fending off questions from the media, asking if the leaks were true. Tomorrow would begin the spin that was the reason for PR minders.

'Why can't you leave government and get a job with one of the big private businesses? They seem desperate for anyone who's worked in government at your level, wanting to know what secrets you have. And they'd pay more–'

They were in the kitchen, saving water by washing up and not using the dishwasher. Water restrictions were tightening as the Big Dry crept in from the west, where many farms were now raising only dust. Brigid and Rosie were in the living room watching *The Simpsons*, learning how to be renegades and loud-mouthed in opinion; their progressive school thought there was no harm in their being exposed to such sedition. Through the kitchen window Leif and Marie caught glimpses of their next-door neighbour, bent almost double, creeping around his garden, holding a hose gingerly in front of him, as if he expected Sydney Water inspectors to leap the fence and catch him in water extravagance.

'Why's he creeping around like that?' asked Leif.

'Why do you think? Monday's a no-watering day.'

'Selfish bugger... Where were we?'

'Look for a job with Big Business, with a capital B. They'd jump at you with your experience–'

'Mar, they work you sixty, seventy hours a

115

week. Two or three nights a week I wouldn't be home–'

'You had to work back Thursday night last week–'

He had been with Dinah, working hard in her bed at her flat. He was not a religious man, but all at once he wondered if his sins, whatever sin was, were catching up with him. 'Once a week, at the most, I work back. I'm comfortable where I am–'

'It'll be a tighter fit if it's just an Office, with a capital O, and not a ministry.' She had an annoying habit of seeing things practically.

He looked out the kitchen window again. The undercover gardener next door, still bent almost double, was waving his sinful hose. Leif, for a moment, had an urge to open the window and yell *Gotcha!* Instead, he turned back to Marie.

'I like working with Steve Perkins. I can manage him. If I went to some big firm, the bosses wouldn't let a PR man manage them.'

She had finished the washing-up, was now setting the table for breakfast. She had a routine about the house that was a contradiction of her sometimes erratic thoughts. She stopped now with the honey and marmalade jars in her hands. 'You're scared, aren't you?'

He was tying up a rubbish bag, preparatory to taking it outside. He, too, paused; for a moment they were as still as store dummies, suddenly strangers. Then he said, 'You don't think much of me, do you? Now all at once you're a big-time writer–'

'Oh, for Crissake!' She almost threw the honey and marmalade jars on the table; one of them rolled and she had to snatch it before it dropped to the floor. 'Jesus, you make me want to throw things at you! For Crissake, get up off your knees and stop feeling sorry for yourself!'

They were interrupted by Brigid suddenly appearing in the kitchen doorway. 'Are you two fighting?'

Marie was quick to recover; in domestic situations women have the quicker wits. 'No, darling. We're – we're just rehearsing what Daddy says will happen in Parliament tomorrow. He's the Government and I'm the Opposition.'

'What's the difference?' asked Brigid, wiser than she knew.

Leif rolled his eyes and took out the garbage. Marie gave the girls a two-minute shower, shared, put them into their pyjamas and took them into their bedroom.

'You *were* fighting,' said Brigid. 'You were swearing, like Granpa does.'

'It was just a tiff, we were arguing about who'd take out the garbage.'

'I think I'll be like Bart,' said Rosie. 'He argues with everyone.'

'Try it, kiddo, and see where you come off.' She kissed them both, leaving the light on for Leif to come in and say goodnight to them.

She and Leif slept that night like strangers in the same bed. Once, asleep, she turned towards him and instinctively put her arm round him; he, awake, gently removed it. Things were no better in the morning. He went off to his office, she took the girls to school, then came home and washed and ironed Leif's shirts, which he did not like being sent to the laundry. At one point she paused, ready to burn a hole in his favourite blue shirt.

He came home early and she knew at once that armistice was in the wind. He was friendly without being apologetic. They had dinner, put the girls to bed, watched some desperate homegrown comics, laughed at the same jokes, then they went to bed.

He came to bed without his usual pyjama pants, all he ever wore, and she slipped out of her nightgown. There were no murmurs of *sorry;* they merged as they always did. She rode him like *Ben Hur,* an old movie she had seen recently on television; the chariot of him beneath her, an imaginary whip cracking, galloping horses between her thighs. When she came she was Ben Hur triumphant. Wisely, wifely, she let him think it was a dead-heat.

3

Enough is enough
  Till more is required...
Steve Perkins quoted it, then said, 'I like it. Who wrote it?'

'I did,' said Leif.

'What's it mean?'

'I dunno. I just typed it, it looked good, so I left it.'

'We'll attribute it to some old Indian philosopher. Do you know any?' Perkins' acquaintance with philosophers, ancient or modern, was nil.

'No, I don't know any. What's the point? Australians can't get their tongue around most Indian names, unless they're cricketers.'

'Well, I'll just say, "As an old Indian philo-

119

sopher once said..."'

'Watch out for that know-it-all on SBS–'

Perkins smiled. He might not know any philosophers, but he knew how to handle smartarse journalists. 'I'll just say I'm sure he knows who I mean and leave it at that...' Then for a moment the light died in his face. 'I'm not looking forward to this.'

'Think like General MacArthur did. *I shall return...*'

'Bullshit.'

It was Wednesday and the demolition of the ministry was about to be announced. The Premier, who announced all *good* news, even the opening of a tent for the homeless, was conveniently out of town for the bad news. Steve Perkins was carrying the can for his own demotion.

'Put on a brave face,' said Leif. 'As an old Indian philosopher once said...'

'Up yours,' said Perkins, but managed to smile. 'It's just like the old days in the union.'

For a disaster, the announcement went off quite well, like the crumbling of a dam wall that held no water. The media scrum, cameras aimed like shotguns, microphones held out like hand grenades, hurled questions, but Perkins, having said his piece, beat his retreat, leaving Leif to answer the questions. He handled it well, keeping his temper, using his experience. These media sessions were a game and he enjoyed them. But not today.

When he returned to his office he called Marie: 'It went better than I expected, but it was still tough. The boss has just told me I stay on at the same salary, but I'll have two less offsiders helping me out. I think things may go okay–'

'I'm glad, sweetheart. Be happy.'

'I'll try. I love you–'

'Same here. Come home and I'll show you how–' She hung up, laughing, and he put down the phone feeling better.

Mid-afternoon he was in his office when Dinah Camplin appeared in the doorway. She was wearing slacks and a white shirt; she looked half-virginal but for the ever-present cleavage. She was carrying a file, the pass-port to all government offices. 'Can I see you?'

'Sure, what's on your mind?' Though he knew. She went to shut the door, but he shook his head. 'Leave it open, it always is.'

She smiled, sat down opposite him across his desk. 'You're afraid of gossip?'

'We've avoided it so far,' he said and

waited. Staff passed by the open door, but didn't look in, unless they had strained their eyes looking sideways.

'They've started making out a list of those who are going to be fired. So far, I'm not on it.'

'You may be lucky. We're keeping a nucleus of staff.' He was glad he was not the one compiling the list.

'I want to come and work for you.'

He took his time, holding in his temper and his unease. 'It wouldn't work, Dinah. There'd be talk before the first day was out–'

'I'm not stupid – I'd be discreet. But I want to stay here, working with you, seeing you each day–'

'Dinah–' He tried to sound patient. 'I'm a married man, you knew that from the beginning–'

'And I'm just your extracurricular fuck?'

He was glad there was no secretary just outside his door. He used the computer pool and now was relieved. 'No, that's not what you are and you know it. But I'm not going to risk my marriage because you want to come and work with me. I'll see what I can do to have you kept on – but not, I repeat *not*, close to me.'

He expected her to erupt, but she didn't;

122

she sat and stared at him for a long moment, the file laid primly on her lap, a cardboard chastity belt. Then she said, 'You're a bastard.'

'Probably. Yes, I am. But you must have guessed that from the beginning–'

'So we're finished?'

He hesitated, unsure of what she would do if he said Yes. None of his other dalliances had presented this problem; the women had recognized them for what they were, casual flings. He said cautiously, 'Let's see–'

She stared at him, her full lips just a tight line. Then she stood up. 'See that Complaints isn't totally abolished, or I'll be a one-woman Complaints section.'

Then she went out of the office, twitching her arse derisively as only a woman can. He picked up his pen, a Mark Cross, a present from Marie when he had first landed this job, and shakily began to write another press release.

Chapter Seven

1

Joe Fernandez was having lunch with Marie's publisher at Machiavelli.

'One goes to Otto's to see who wants to be noticed in Sydney,' said Nigel Panopoulos. 'But you come here to see who runs Sydney.'

Joe looked around the restaurant, recognizing some of the other diners. There were many more men than women; never let it be said that the glass ceiling was melting. The waiters moved amongst the diners like old retainers. Power flavoured every dish that was served. Joe looked back at his host:

'Mr Panopoulos–'

'Nigel, please.'

'Nigel? Nigel Panopoulos?' Somewhere Zeus and the Greek gods were laughing.

'My mother is English. She came out here years ago, she was a film editor, to work on a film that folded after two days. She met my father, he was a soundman, and they married. Five offspring. My brother Alistair and me. Three sisters – Athena, Dione and Chloe. All Greek goddesses according to my father. Unfortunately, I'm not a Greek god.' He smiled, comfortable in his stoutness and his bald head. 'We celebrate the Queen's birthday and all the Greek festival days. One of my sisters is married to an Iranian, a computer whiz, and another to an American, a TV reporter. We're looking for an Australian for Chloe. Are you single?'

'Divorced. And I was born in Spain, so I'm not a true-blue Aussie.'

He was always patient, leaving clients or adversaries to get down to business. He had an Arab client who thought circumlocution was the best way to a direct point, and a Chinese client who smiled at even the worst of news. Nigel Panopoulos, half-English, half-Greek, knew where the money lay.

Panopoulos smiled. 'I think you and I are going to get along, Joe. We're birds of a feather.'

'Well, let's get to the point. How's Marie's book, doing?'

'It's in its third printing, each one bigger than the last. And we're already getting ready for a fourth.'

'I've seen the contract–'

'She still hasn't signed it. Women can be so lax.'

That's the Greek in him, thought Joe.

'And what's with the foreign publishers?'

'Just as enthused as we are. The Americans want Marie to go to the States for an author tour. She's a good-looker, she's bright – I can see her holding her own with Oprah. Persuade her to say yes – she's saying no to us, says she can't leave her kids. What's her husband like?'

'As a child-minder? Hopeless.'

'She has a sister, a good-looking woman. I saw her at the book launch.'

'My ex-wife.'

Panopoulos smiled. 'I know. We also publish detective novels.'

'She's not a babysitter. She has a good job and she seems pretty happy the way she is... What's happening on the TV movie?'

'It may get bigger, the Americans are talking of making it into something like the old Ealing comedies. You know them? No? My mother treasures them. Things are looking better and better, Joe.'

'Maybe we can re-work the contract, give Marie a better percentage.'

Panopoulos shook his head. 'Not a hope. We're owned by a British-German conglomerate whose only editorial interest is the bottom line.'

'Tell 'em you're dealing with a Spaniard whose line goes back to the Inquisition. And my old man was a picador, very efficient with the lance.'

Panopoulos smiled again. 'Are you advising Marie on where to invest all her money?'

'Yes.'

Panopoulos looked at him shrewdly. 'You're pretty involved in this.'

Joe nodded. 'More than I expected.' He had been aware that he had stepped into the shallows of an emotional sea that Marie (and Leif, probably) were not certain of. With his legal clients he was accustomed to emotion, but it was usually bitter and not euphoric. He came back to business, where he always kept emotion under control: 'The contract hasn't yet been signed.'

'No, but it's just a formality.'

Joe shook his head. 'No, she won't be signing it. I've drawn up a new one.' He nodded at the briefcase on the third chair at their table. 'You get none of the overseas and TV deals, you get only Australian and New Zealand rights.'

Panopoulos paused with a forkful of terrine to his mouth. He looked at it, then put it down as if it had suddenly gone sour. A waiter appeared like a genie: 'Something wrong, Mr Panopoulos?'

'No, no.' Panopoulos shook his head. 'I just bit my tongue.' The waiter uttered a word of sympathy and went away. Panopoulos looked at Joe: 'You can't do that–'

'Nigel,' said Joe, munching *his* terrine with relish, 'I've done it. Your Brit-German bosses had better get used to a new bottom line.'

'We won't agree–'

'Nigel, you can't *dis*agree. Marie owns all the foreign rights and the TV and film rights. It's right there in the contract I've drawn up.' He nodded again at his briefcase. 'You're committed, you've published three editions and you're going into a fourth. How many more will come your way? Be satisfied with what you've got.'

Panopoulos picked up his fork again. 'Marie should have warned me against you.'

'She didn't know what a bastard I can be.' He looked around the restaurant again; he saw two Cabinet ministers, a top banker whom he recognized from the financial pages, a Supreme Court judge, a radio jock who had more influence than the Cabinet ministers. He looked back at his host.

'Machiavelli. I feel quite at home here.'

'Indeed,' said Nigel Panopoulos, but had the grace to smile.

2

The next night Joe invited himself to dinner at the Johnsons'. He took along a bottle of Pol Roger. With his legal clients he never provided a celebratory drink: it was up to them to deliver champagne, beer or water. In this new territory, as a part-time literary agent, he felt an uncommon extravagance.

While Marie prepared the dinner, he sat with Leif and Brigid and Rosie, who were in their pyjamas, ready for bed. He liked the two girls and they liked him: he was their Uncle Joe. He looked at them and occasionally imagined a third figure with them; had it not been for the miscarriage, his and Louise's child, a boy, would have been four years old. Like Brigid and Rosie, becoming a personality.

Leif, sitting between the two girls on a couch, said, 'How's business?'

'Fine. Divorces are increasing, almost at the same rate as people are dying.'

'What's divorce?' asked Rosie.

Brigid rolled her eyes, the way smart kids on TV did. 'It's when–'

Leif interrupted. 'Uncle Joe and I are talking. Don't interrupt.'

'Well, Uncle Joe and Auntie Lou are divorced–'

Leif looked at Joe. 'What can I do with them?'

Joe grinned. There were times when he wondered what sort of talk he would have had with his son. What would they have talked about, what questions would the boy have asked? He looked at Brigid and Rosie and said, 'What should we do with you?'

But Leif silenced them before they could quote a list. 'Just be quiet for a while. I'm talking to Uncle Joe.'

'How are things working out now the ministry's been dumped?'

Leif shrugged. 'It means less work for me, even though I've lost two of my staff. My boss is now the Minister for Bits and Pieces and he's finding it hard to adapt. But we'll survive.'

Then Marie came to the door. 'Okay, girls, time for bed. Say goodnight to Uncle Joe.'

He kissed the girls, then on an impulse hugged them both. He looked up between them at Marie. Her face was expressionless, then she nodded. *She understands*, he thought.

Dinner was pleasant and relaxed. There was roast chicken, baked potatoes and carrots; the dessert was *baba au rhum*. Marie was an experimental cook, but she knew that Joe liked old-fashioned dishes. They finished the Pol Roger and Leif brought out a brandy. Joe, without looking around, took it all in. This was middle-class solidity: the meal, the furnishings, the house itself. And it was all about to be invaded by fortune.

Over coffee Joe poured fortune on Marie and Leif: 'I've brought the new contract for you to sign. You own everything outside of Australia and New Zealand. It's all yours.'

'Have you got any idea how much it'll all add up to?' asked Leif.

Joe shrugged. 'Your guess is as good as mine.'

'I was reading that the new Harry Potter, the first printing in America is going to be eight or nine million. Whew!'

'Come back to earth,' said Marie. 'That's the stratosphere, we're back here on earth.'

Leif sipped his brandy. 'I know – but one can dream–'

'And you're good at that,' she said and leaned across and kissed him. Then she looked at Joe and smiled. 'Excuse us. He needs encouraging.'

'They want Marie to go on an author tour in the States,' said Leif. 'That would help, wouldn't it? I'm trying to persuade her, the girls and I could go with her–'

'Leif, it wouldn't work. I talked with Nigel Panopoulos yesterday. A book tour is a real grind. It could be a breakfast interview in New York, a midday one in Boston, a late night one in Chicago. You fancy traipsing the kids around after her like that? Stay home and count the money as it rolls in – we hope.'

Marie got up, came round the table and kissed him. 'I'm glad someone has his feet on the ground.'

Joe looked at Leif, who grinned sheepishly and said, 'She wins. She always does.'

Marie went round, kissed him, then sat down again. 'What worries me now, is what do I write next? My editor has suggested a sequel to Barney and his mates, but I'm empty of any ideas. I may turn out to be a one-book success.'

'Enjoy it,' said Joe and wondered how hard that would be for her. One of his clients had been a would-be rock star who had had one hit record, then faded away like a guitar with broken strings. Success was an unreliable medication.

He drove home through an autumn night still tinged with summer; the seasons, it seemed, were as unstable as the world itself. He put his car away in the garage at the back of the mansion, went inside and climbed the wide stairs, hand on the polished oak stair-rail, to his flat. He had insisted that, when the big house was being remodelled for commercial as well as private use, that as much as possible be retained of the original. He valued the past, even though he was not a native.

His flat was large, with big rooms, high ceilings and deep windows. He had furnished it with antiques bought at auctions. The dining room table and the eight chairs were from the 1890s; one could imagine walrus-moustached men and women with piled-up hair as ghosts round the table. The only modern piece in the Edwardian living room was the television set, looking as out of place as a fast-food billboard in a church. The kitchen had an electric stove, a double-oven and a microwave, but the room itself was all timber-lined and the kitchen table was a nineteenth-century relic. The two bedrooms were in keeping with the rest of the flat and would have put off any woman not wearing a bustle; the large bed in the main bedroom was a four-poster with a canopy. The only modern room in the flat was the bathroom, but even the door to it was an antique. It was not a bachelor's pad, but a home waiting for a family.

Joe went to bed, lay on his back for a while, suddenly lonely. When he went to sleep he dreamed of a woman who *felt* familiar but whose face he couldn't see.

Chapter Eight

1

Louise was summoned to the office of the assistant general manager. She had been expecting the call because all the other section supervisors had been reporting upstairs for the past week. She left the Chapelli counter to Mira, went across to the lifts and rode up to the eighth floor.

The lift-driver, grey and grizzled, had been going up and down for fifty years. He looked at Louise and grinned without opening his lips. 'I feel like one of them tumbril drivers, you know from the French Revolution. You getting the chop?'

'I hope not, Barry. What about you?'

'I leave Friday week. Fifty years and I think I'll be glad to go. From then on youse drive yourselves up and down.'

'Pretty soon, the world won't need workers.'

He nodded. 'Eighth floor. Good luck, Louise.'

'You, too, Barry.'

The assistant general manager was Nola Greenfield. She was fortyish, power-suited in black, and her blonde head was pressed hard against the glass ceiling. Everyone knew that some day she would be Chief Executive, something she, too, knew, but which didn't make her unlikeable.

'Sit down, Louise,' she said and got straight to the point: 'How's business with Chapelli?'

'Slow, but it always is with winter coming on.'

Ms Greenfield looked at the file in front of her. 'I'm not blaming you, Louise, but the figures for the past month are well down. I'm afraid there's going to have to be a change.'

Louise stiffened without moving. 'How?'

'There'll be no bonus for the next three months. And you are going to lose – what's your assistant's name?'

'Mira. She's going to be sacked?'

'No, we'll move her to another department.'

Pawns on a checkerboard; she and Joe had once played the game. 'I'm safe?'

The blonde head nodded. 'You're an asset on that counter, Louise. Our male customers obviously respond.'

Sounds as if I'm running a brothel. 'May I make a suggestion about Mira? Put her in the up-market men's department. She knows how to sell to men.'

Ms Greenfield smiled. 'So do you... Okay, we'll see how – Mira? – goes. Can you handle Chapelli on your own? Good. It's tough, Louise, but we've got to face facts. DJs and Myer are having four and five sales a year now. We're not going to attempt that for the time being, but it may come to it. The buying public are at last waking up to how big their credit card debt is. Do you use your card a lot?'

'Only in emergencies,' said Louise piously.

'Well, let's see how things go... I saw your sister's book down in the book department – they tell me it's selling like hot cakes.'

'Maybe I should be transferred to the book department?' But she smiled as she said it.

So did Ms Greenfield. 'You'd be wasted, Louise. Men are not great book-buyers.'

Louise went back to the ground floor and gave Mira the bad news. Mira was upset at first, but soon accepted the transfer; she was an optimist who looked for the silver lining in even the most leaden situation. There would be better prospects in Men's Up-

Market than in Women's Larger Sizes.

That evening Louise went to dinner with one of her gay male friends. They went to an Italian restaurant in Leichhardt, where Italians seemed to make up most of the population. Rob Loomis *looked* Italian and the waitress, the granddaughter of a *capo* in Salerno, gave him all her attention while ignoring Louise.

When the waitress had gone away with their orders, Louise said, 'You've made a conquest there. Why aren't you heterosexual, Rob? What a world!'

She had known him twelve months, but had never raised the question before.

'Women would line up for you–'

He was handsome, well-built, charming: everything a woman could hope for. He smiled as if he had been asked the question a hundred times; not bored, just amused. 'I tried it once or twice when I was a teenager. It was a disaster. I'd suspected for a year or two that I was gay. It was a bit of a shock, but it didn't floor me. When my mother and father found out, it floored *them*.'

'Have they come to accept it now?' She knew how her own father felt about gays: not derisive, but uncomfortable when the subject was brought up. Joe had always accepted homosexuality as a human trait, some had it, some didn't, but she had never mentioned Rob Loomis to him.

'Oddly enough, Dad got over it much quicker than I'd expected. He was uncomfortable about it for a while, with his friends at the golf club – they were all as straight as a Number 7 iron–' He smiled again, shook his head. 'I have two sisters, both older than me. Happily married, one with three boys, the other has two. Mum wanted me to marry and present her with a granddaughter or two. But she's accepted me now. Occasionally I take home a friend for dinner and everything goes smoothly. Sometimes I feel I've let her down,' he said, not smiling.

'What would happen if you took me home?' said Louise teasingly.

He had the most charming smile; the waitress, passing, almost dropped a tray. 'Mum would hang out bunting on the front door and Dad would probably make a pass at you.'

Then the waitress came back with their first course, which she placed with ceremony in front of him and gave a backhand serve to Louise. She went away, her hips inviting him to follow her, and Louise looked after her.

'Why is it that Mediterranean women know how to swing their hips?'

He smiled again. 'Have you ever walked up Oxford Street and seen how the hips swing there? All male and very few of them from Italy.'

'Have you got a partner now?' She hadn't seen him for a couple of months.

He shook his head again. 'I'm like you, Lou. At a loose end.' He stopped eating and looked at her. He could be amazingly sympathetic and that was one reason she always enjoyed seeing him. 'You are, aren't you?'

She took her time, then nodded. 'I think it's happening more and more with women. We've achieved freedom, of a sort. But so what? For women of a certain age it's like running around loose in an empty paddock.'

'Very literary. It must run in the family.' He went back to his prawn *linguini;* he ate with relish, like an Italian. 'Be, careful, Lou.'

'You, too,' she said.

He took her home in his late-model Alfa-Romeo, the leather still smelling new. He worked for an investment bank and, she guessed, earned at least three times what she brought home. He was everything a woman wanted, on the surface, but she knew she would never be able to get round the bend on gender. She could enjoy sex without love, but she couldn't imagine love without sex.

He drove with flair, manipulating the manual gears like a musician, and for a moment she thought of asking him to take her away for a weekend in the mountains, separate rooms, of course, but she restrained herself.

But when they pulled up outside her flat she leaned across and kissed him. 'Come up and I'll rape you.'

He didn't smile. He looked at her as if not sure whether she was serious or not. Then he said, and sounded apologetic, 'You'd be disappointed, Lou. I'd be dead meat. I'm not fluid, double-gaited, like some of them.'

She sat back, looked at him tenderly. 'Are you unhappy, Rob?'

He shrugged. 'Sometimes. More lonely than unhappy.'

'Be careful, Rob. Don't get into something that's second or third choice.'

'You neither, Lou,' he said. 'You be careful, too.'

When she went upstairs there was a voice-mail from Joe: 'My mother and father are coming down Saturday, they're bringing your dad. I'm putting on a barbecue. Drinks at midday, sausages at one. Come, Lou.'

She went to bed feeling as lonely as women of a certain age.

2

Over the next two days on the Chapelli counter she sold a watch, two bottles of perfume and a pair of earrings, not enough to cover the overheads. The ground floor was almost deserted, looking like a glass icefield; the chandeliers were frozen suns. The organist on the Wurlitzer played sad songs from the 1930s; all the floor staff listened, wondering if it was medieval music. The *Herald* on the Friday morning said the country was pulling its belt in. All that was rising were the viewing figures for *Desperate Housewives*. That and petrol prices.

She and Mira alternated for Saturday duty and tomorrow would be Mira's last day exposed to the approaches of predatory rich men. 'My mum is glad I'm going to menswear, she thinks I could get into trouble here.'

'How many propositions have you had?' Louise had had at least half a dozen, all veiled as innocent *tête-à-têtes*.

Mira smiled ruefully. 'None so far. Well,

one. But he was fat and old, he must've been sixty at least.'

'Ancient,' said Louise. 'Good luck in menswear. Offer to measure their inside leg, that's a good come-on.'

'You have a lovely dirty mind,' said Mira.

Saturday morning Louise took her laundry to a nearby laundrette, read all the bad news in the paper while she waited, accidentally turned to the sports pages and read that Tiger Woods had earned another million or two, gave up and took the washing out of the machine. She carried it home; the ironing could be done tomorrow. She then took a duster and went through the flat rearranging the dust so that her cleaning lady, who came in for two hours every Monday, would not think she was a slattern. Then it was time to go to Joe's barbecue.

She showered, then looked at herself in a full-length mirror. Everything was where it should be: her breasts were still firm, her belly flat and her bum still tight. She debated whether to put on an expensive perfume (bought at a discount), but decided it would be wasted against the smell of sizzling sausages and steak. She put on a yellow sweater and black slacks and threw a matching yellow cardigan over her shoulders. She looked at herself again in the mirror, decided she looked just fine – but for whom?

On her way to Strathfield in the Barina she stopped off and bought a bottle of good shiraz (Joe, since their divorce, was developing into a wine snob), then drove on, enjoying the day and the prospect of whatever lay ahead. She parked her car in Joe's driveway, amongst half a dozen other cars, then walked round the side of the house to the large back garden where Joe held his barbecues.

He came towards her at once, bringing a girl with him, took the bottle of wine, said, 'This is Sharon', and went away. She was sure that he was leering.

The girl was attractive, with a thick mane of dark auburn hair that Louise, experienced in the roots of truth, saw was a dye job, but a good one. She, too, wore a yellow sweater, tighter than Louise's, dark green slacks and the air of a girl who knew she had a good figure and here it was, boys.

'He's a nice man,' said Sharon, looking after the disappearing Joe.

'Yes. Have you known him long?' Probing, like a private eye in a divorce case. *What's the matter with me?*

'Only casually.' She managed to make

144

casually sound like *intimately.* 'I'm the receptionist for Dr Kosta.' The GP on the floor below Joe's office. 'Are you a relation?'

'Sort of,' said Louise, chewing the words like candy. 'I'm his ex-wife.'

'Oh.' She sounded deflated; even the breasts under the tight sweater seemed to lose bulk. 'He didn't warn me.'

'He never does,' said Louise, sharpening her knife before the steak and sausages were ready. 'Relax – Sharon? We're just good friends now, that's all.'

'He's very friendly,' said Sharon, regaining some of her composure.

'I taught him.'

Then Joe's mother, Isabella, came in on the run and flung her arms round Louise. Sharon stepped back, then nodded at Louise and drifted away. Isabella let go of Louise and looked after the tight green slacks.

'Who's she?'

'She works here, for the doctor. She might be Joe's latest.' But she smiled as she said it, teasing Isabella, whom she loved as a stand-in mother. 'Don't worry, Bella. He's not going to elope with her.'

'Her trousers are too tight, she's showing off her *trasera.* Like a matador.'

Louise smiled. 'Didn't Hernando show off

145

his *trasera?*'

'He was on a horse, so it was spread over a saddle. It wasn't his *trasera* I fell in love with. I was in love with him when he was just fourteen and skinny all over.'

Then the ex-picador, *sans* horse, arrived. 'Turn around, Hernando,' said Louise.

'What for?' He looked at his wife.

'She wants to see what your *tasero* looks like.'

'She's going in for that?' But he pivoted slowly, flashing a perfect set of false teeth. He was not a handsome man, but women looked at him because he looked at them. Yet Louise had never heard Isabella complain about his straying. Like Joe, he was an old-fashioned moralist.

Isabella, a social mixer, went off to mix, and Louise and Hernando sat down on a garden seat. He was still a good figure of a man and he wore clothes with panache; he even wore a cravat today, tucked into the V of his dark-blue sweater. Joe, though not sloppy, had never had his father's flair.

He looked at Louise and said without flattery, 'You're still beautiful, Louise.' He always called her by her full name. 'Why did my stupid son let you go?'

'It wasn't his fault. It just happened – I

guess we were both to blame. These things happen, Nando. You and Isabella are lucky to have lasted so long.'

He considered that, then nodded. 'Yes. We were sweethearts when we were just kids back in Benidorm.'

'Do you ever get homesick, want to go back?'

He shook his head, rubbed his hand over his thinning grey thatch. 'We get homesick, both of us, but we'd never go back. When we lived there, we were both born there, Benidorm was just starting to grow. It had been a large fishing village and there were a few lock-up apartments owned by middle-class Madridenos, they'd come down in the summer. Now–' He shook his head again. 'My brother sends us photos. It is the largest resort in Europe, has four-and-a-half million visitors a year. Isabella calls it Miami on the Mediterranean. We could never go back. Benidorm, for us, isn't there any more.'

Louise wondered how many natives, especially those on the Central Coast, where Hernando and Isabella now lived, resented the influx of outsiders, the overdevelopment of a coastline that had once been as Benidorm must have been. But she did not raise the subject with Hernando.

He looked past her, was alone for a moment. Then he went on: 'Life was no picnic under Franco, not for us. But he couldn't touch the past, we always had that to look back to. The long-ago past,' he said and focussed his gaze on her again. 'You're lucky, Louise.'

She understood what he meant: her roots were *here*. 'Did you always want to be a bullfighter?'

'Always. The nearest *corrida* was at Alicante, 25 kilometres down the coast, and every Sunday my father and I would catch the bus down there. Then I went to a bullfighters' school–'

'Did you wear – what did they call it?' She had heard Joe once describe it.

'A suit of lights? No, they're only for matadors. They told me I was not graceful, not athletic enough to be a matador. So they put me on a horse and made me a picador. I was a good one, never out of work. Barcelona, Madrid, Seville–' For a moment he was back in the long-ago: the cities rolled off his tongue like shrines. Then he looked past her. 'Here comes the Happy Hour. He never stopped complaining all the way down in the car.'

Matt Micklethwaite, hobbling on a stick,

sat down on Louise's other side and grinned. 'Only about his driving. What sort of Spanish bull has he been feeding you?'

Hernando stood, kissed the top of Louise's head. 'Be happy, *querida*,' he said and walked away, a toreador with nothing more to fight than memories.

'Well, how are you?' Louise asked her father. 'How's Dr Teddes?'

'Still round the bend. He's now advising us to invest in blood pressure, says it's sure to rise. He brought his son with him this week, most contradictory bugger I've ever met.'

'Why, what does he do?'

'Makes wigs. He's always splitting hairs.' There was a gurgle of laughter in his throat and he looked at her out of the corner of his eye.

She whacked him, but gently. His jokes were often poor, but she knew he preferred to weep with laughter than with sorrow.

Then he said, not joking, 'I sometimes think Hernando is unhappy. Are you?'

She thought about it, then said, 'No. Lonely sometimes. Like you.'

He nodded, saying nothing.

She looked away, saw Sharon in the distance, hovering close to Joe like an incestuous mother-hen. Then she looked back at her father. 'Did you ever look at other women besides Mum?'

He looked a little surprised at the question, but then he grinned. 'Plumbers spend ninety per cent of their time with women, the husbands are never there. Of course I looked, but when you're flat on your back under an S-bend pipe it's hard to go any further.'

She put up her hand and fondled the back of his neck. 'Mum would've S-bended your neck if you had.'

Then the Johnsons arrived. Marie, all her life, had *arrived*; Brigid and Rosie had inherited the talent. They came in in a rush, like human floodwater, and everyone, laughing, peeled back to make way for them. Leif, laughing at them as he always did, came in behind them, like backwash. Brigid and Rosie flung themselves at their aunt and grandfather. Louise hugged them to her, looking between their heads at Joe, in a butcher's apron, over at the barbecue stove. Sharon was beside him, poking delicately at the sausages and steak as if the meat was still on the hoof. Joe looked towards her, but he was too far away for her to read the expression, if any, on his face.

150

Then it was eating time. Louise stood in line to be served her steak and sausage, potato with sour cream and her salad. Sharon was on the salad bowl, a hostess-in-training.

'Enjoying yourself?' said Louise, tasting malice as an appetiser.

'Oh yes,' said Sharon. 'A barbecue is a great social leveller, don't you think?'

She's not as dumb as I thought. 'Oh, you said it! We couldn't be leveller, could we?'

Sharon looked at her, salad fork and spoon held like weapons. 'Just what I said to Joe.'

Joe Fernandez's barbecues were not occasions where you stood around or sat on the grass. He had hired or borrowed tables and chairs. Louise sat at a table with Marie and Leif. Not far away Brigid and Rosie were with their grandfather and Hernando and Isabella. Louise, eyes sharpened, waited to see where Joe and Sharon would sit.

'Is that Joe's new girlfriend?' asked Leif.

'She could be.' Even in her own ears Louise's voice sounded as dry as week-old crust.

Leif looked at her, but said nothing.

'Where'd he find her?' Marie, discarding fork and knife, was holding up a sausage.

'Below him,' said Louise and for a moment wanted to leave it at that. Then she

151

added, 'She's the doctor's receptionist.'

Then she saw Joe take Sharon across to sit with his parents, Matt and the girls. She sat between the girls, who, juvenile match-makers, looked her up and down as new goods. Joe patted the girls' heads, said something to them, then, plate loaded, came across and sat down with the Johnsons and Louise.

'That your new girlfriend?' said Marie, lobbing a grenade.

'She's on approval,' said Joe and grinned at Louise. 'How'd you get on with her?'

'Fine – till I mentioned I was your ex-wife. That took the wind out of her sweater.'

'I hadn't noticed,' said Joe, still grinning, and she knew then that Sharon was no competition. And wondered at her own selfishness, since Joe was no longer hers.

'You two are still together,' said Marie, watching them. 'Even if you're apart.'

'Why don't you mind your own business?' said Leif, but his voice wasn't sharp and he winked at Joe.

'Just what I was about to say,' said Louise.

Joe reached for the bottle of wine Louise had brought, poured himself a glass. 'The world goes round,' he said, took a sip of wine. 'Sometimes you find yourself in tandem. It may not last, but there you are. Right, love?'

Bugger you, thought Louise. But she nodded. 'Yes.'

'Which proves my point,' said Marie. 'Up to a point.'

'I'll never understand women,' said Leif, but didn't look in the least put out.

'You can say that again,' said Marie and Louise.

'Do you understand them, Joe?' asked Leif. 'You must meet all sorts in the legal game.'

But Joe just looked at Louise, then back at Leif and shook his head. 'Did Adam understand Eve?'

Later when it was time to leave, Louise went across to her father. She paused for a moment before she got to him, looked at him sitting alone, hands clasped on his walking-stick. He suddenly looked old and shrunken and she felt a surge of love and pity for him. He and her mother had been the ideal couple, as close as it was possible to be, and when Norah had died half his life had gone with her. He had kept his grief to himself, always hidden behind his gruff complaints as to what was wrong with the rest of the world. But now, sitting alone, Louise saw the truth of him.

Then he looked up, saw her, grinned and was several years younger. 'I've been thinking about young Brigid and Rosie. It's gunna be tougher for them, later on, than it was for you and Marie. Or me and Mum.'

'Marie should be able to take care of them. Money-wise, school and university, things like that.'

'Money-wise won't be the answer. Or the problem. It'll be the way things have changed. People don't have the values we used to have.'

'Have you read Mar's book?'

'Sure. And I liked it. Kids robbing banks, I'm all for it.'

'Who's talking old values now?'

He ignored that. 'It isn't real, but it's more real than fantasy. I never had any time for fantasy. I read a book from our library, it was about an Oxford don, I've forgotten his name but he was well known. Once a month he'd have a dinner at his place for six or eight other dons. Then they'd all head for his study and a port and a smoke. The drill was that one of them, they were all writers of some sort, poets, historians, all types, the drill was that they took it in turns to read from what they called a work in progress. One night it was JRR Tolkien's turn. He stood up, and said something like, "You all know I'm working on a novel about a place called Middle Earth. This week I've introduced some new characters." And some bloke over in a corner said, "Oh God, not another effing elf!" And that's the way I feel about fantasy. Give me kids robbing banks any time.'

She kissed his forehead. 'There are about twenty million people around the world who'd beat you to death, they heard you say that.'

'They wouldn't be game. They'd send in the effing elves.'

'Well, don't you worry about Brigid and Rosie. Mar's not going to spoil them.'

'It's not her I'm worried about. It's what's outside.'

Then Hernando came across to them. 'Time to be going, Matt. You got all your complaints ready for the trip back?'

Matt stood up, seeming to creak, and grinned at Louise. 'The wages of age.'

'Not as good as the wages of sin,' said Hernando.

'I can't remember what sin was.'

They were old men's jokes. They went off, one leaning on the other, voters in territory that the young still had to come to know.

Louise looked around. Most of the guests were departing; goodbyes, take-cares, filled the air. People waved to Louise and she waved back. She had a sudden empty feeling that the day was falling apart. Then she mentally kicked herself for her self-pity; she looked after her father, someone much lonelier than herself. *Snap out of it, Lou.*

She went across to where Joe was cleaning the barbecue stove. Marie and Leif were tidying up, taking the dirty paper plates to a nearby rubbish bin. Then Leif, accompanied by the girls ('I wanna go to the toilet!'), took a basket loaded with glasses up into the house. Louise and Marie were left alone with Joe.

'Where's Sharon?' asked Louise.

Joe smiled at Marie. 'She's busting to know... She's upstairs in the kitchen washing up the cutlery.'

'She's domesticated,' Louise said to Marie. 'That's nice. He knows how to pick 'em. You think she scrubs floors?'

'I wonder if she darns socks?' said Marie.

Joe just grinned, scraped fat off the hotplate.

Then Sharon came out of the house and across to them. She said to Marie, 'I met your husband, Reef–'

'Leif,' said Marie. 'He has a lisp.'

Sharon wasn't fazed. 'He seems a lovely man. And the children, too.'

'They're well-trained,' said Marie. 'All three of them.'

'You like children?' said Louise sweetly. 'You'd like to be a mother?'

'Not yet awhile,' said Sharon just as sweetly. 'I'd have to select the father first.'

Joe, head down, was polishing the barbecue stove as if it were sterling silver.

'Joe tells me you've written a book,' said Sharon, making it sound as if Marie had produced another child.

'Yes,' said Marie.

'It's going to be a big seller,' said Louise, suddenly a PR agent. 'A children's book, but about real kids. She's Enid Blyton with balls, isn't that right, Joe?'

Joe uttered what sounded like a sigh, gave up looking for his reflection in the hotplate, straightened up. 'I'll suggest they use that on the dust jacket. It'll go down well in the UK.'

Suddenly Louise was tired of the fencing. 'I'm going,' she said, kissed Marie, blew Joe a kiss, smiled at Sharon and went looking for Leif and Brigid and Rosie. She found them in the flat. Entering it she realized it was the first time she had seen it. She had had dinner with Joe and he had occasionally come to her flat, but (and she wondered why) he had never invited her here. It was as if, now they were apart, he was keeping some of himself private.

She looked around and Leif, coming out of another room, said, 'It's, I dunno, it's *Joe*. Solid, old-fashioned–'

'Don't be nasty–'

'I'm not. In a way I envy him. He's the solidest of all four of us. You and me included,' he said and gave her a direct stare, almost challengingly.

She had been surprised at how she had completely washed him out of herself. *Washed? Well, yes.* She still felt shame at what she had done to Marie and would go on feeling it; that would never be washed out of her. 'You're probably right–'

Then Brigid and Rosie came in from the main bedroom, saving the day. 'Have you seen Uncle Joe's bedroom? Fantastic! It's like in them old-fashioned pictures, you know, the ones with queens in bed! Rosie and I wanna come and stay here!'

'Fantastic!' said Rosie. 'Come and have a look, Auntie Lou!'

She grabbed Louise's hand and led her

into the main bedroom. Louise looked around; it was so unlike the bedroom in her Abbotsford flat. Against her will she wondered how many women he had brought here to this bed with its four posts and its elaborate fringed canopy. *How many queens had he laid here?*

'Let's bounce up and down on it,' said Brigid, and she and Rosie clambered up onto the bed and began to bounce, shrieking with laughter. Louise spun round and flung herself back on the bed with them, laughing, while Leif stood just inside the doorway, smiling and shaking his head at them.

Then Louise saw Joe, still in his butcher's apron, come into the room behind Leif. She suddenly stopped laughing, put restraining hands on the girls on either side of her and sat up.

'Does a man have no privacy?' His voice rasped, exactly as he had sounded, unexpectedly, in the last argument they had had before they broke up.

She flushed, embarrassed in front of the girls and Leif. She slid off the bed and Leif, voice terribly sober, said, 'Okay, girls, time we were going. Get off the bed.'

Louise looked directly at Joe. 'I'm sorry – the girls and I–' But her throat was dry, she ran out of words.

Joe looked at the girls, seemed to force a smile. 'I'm sorry, Brigid, Rosie – I didn't mean to be snarly – I'm tired–'

'We all are,' said Leif, gathering the girls to him. 'It's time we went home.'

Brigid seemed aware of the changed atmosphere, but Rosie said, 'Can we come again, Uncle Joe, and bounce on the bed? It's fantastic!'

'Any time, love,' said Joe and rubbed the top of her head. Then he looked at Louise and dug up a smile: 'You, too.'

'I'm sorry, Joe,' she said and pushed past him and Leif and went out of the flat, feeling as if she had been stripped in front of a stranger.

She went home to Abbotsford, driving cautiously because she was still tumbling inside. She went up into the flat, threw herself on her own, uncanopied bed and wept, suddenly more lonely than she had ever felt.

Several hours later, after staring listlessly at television, eating peanuts and sipping some white wine, she was getting ready for bed when the phone rang. It was Joe.

'I've been debating whether to call you–'

She looked at her watch: it was 9.50. 'Joe, I said I was sorry–'

160

It was as if he hadn't heard her: 'Lou, why are you still jealous?'

She was shocked: 'I'm not! What put that into–'

'Lou–' He sounded his usual patient self; patience in others can be chafing. 'You were always jealous–'

'Oh, for Crissake–'

'You were, love. I can remember–' He cited an instance, as if reading from a diary, that she had no memory of. 'It irritated me back then, but I never said anything–'

'Joe–' She tried to sound patient; arguments over the phone are handicapped because there are no visuals to them; you are arguing with a voice, not a face or a body. 'I was bitchy this afternoon, but I wasn't *jealous*. I dunno why, but I just fell into a bad mood–'

Joe laughed, dry as a rattle in his throat. 'I'm not going to argue, Lou. But don't get yourself stirred up because you see me with another woman. I'm old enough to run my own life,' he said and hung up.

Louise went to bed unhappy and unstable. She realized that, though divorced from him, Joe had been a rock on whom she depended.

Chapter Nine

1

Marie was being interviewed by Charmaine Charleston and she had better be aware of the honour. Ms Charleston was a busty blonde leaning over backwards not to reach middle age. She was dressed in a figure-clinging knitted suit, her black boots reached to her knee and her helmet of hair looked as if it could defy an axe. She was Channel 15's biggest star, the *doyenne* of morning chat shows. She never appeared after dark, at least not on television. Channel 15's evening programmes were aimed at the under-35s and there was no room for Charmaine in that category. Demography had widened from statistics on mere birth, death and disease to reaction to pulp TV.

'And you were looking for moral values when you wrote the book?' Moral values had become the new catchcry, as if history had known only immoral values.

'No, not really–' Then Marie saw her publishers' PR girl, beside the camera, vigorously shaking her head. 'Well, not till I had the story shaped in my mind. Then I tried to get across, subtly, that crime doesn't pay.' She couldn't believe what she was saying, but she managed to keep a straight face. 'It doesn't, you know.'

'Oh, of course. You think that your readers, say about eleven or twelve, you think that they might already be showing criminal tendencies?'

'No – no–'

The PR girl's head was moving violently from shoulder to shoulder, like an Indian temple dancer gone berserk. Beside her the cameraman was grinning, tempted to swing the camera onto her.

Marie struggled for words: 'It's never too soon to encourage, er, moral values. Why, they're giving sex education to children now when they're only eight or nine.'

'I understand you have two little girls. Do you give them sex education?'

'Only about the birds and the bees,' said Marie sweetly. Somehow she got through the rest of the interview. She had never been shy, but now, all at once, she felt *exposed*. Despite her open attitude to life there had always been a part of her that was private.

Don't enter here, the sign had said; though no one had ever had cause to read it. Not even Leif. But she had just exposed herself, or part of herself, to God knew how many viewers out there at the end of the TV beam.

'That was fantastic,' said Charmaine Charleston; then looked at the studio manager with his clipboard. 'Who's next?'

Marie, legs a little wobbly, followed Biddy Grant, the PT& girl, out of the studio to the parking lot. 'How do you think I went?'

'You survived her. You'll have a breeze with the others we've got lined up.'

Biddy was a pretty blonde with long hair; Marie had recently seen a photograph of twenty-four girls lined up for an audition, twenty-two of them blondes with long hair. Scandinavia had slipped south of the equator. But Biddy was no dumb blonde, she had the publicity game divided and subdivided.

'We're on our way now to a book-signing. You'll be asked to autograph it to Emily or Tracey-Anne or Charlene-Darlene and you'll do it all with a smile and a legible autograph, not one of those illegible scrawls that tennis players hand out. Then we have an ABC radio interview this afternoon. Wednesday we fly down to Melbourne for the day, you're on Bert Newton and we have three other interviews lined up. It's all go, go, go, Marie.'

'Do other authors have to do this?'

'Successful ones, yes. The book trade these days is a cut-throat game. My grandfather owned a bookstore years ago and he said it was a gentleman's game. Not any more.' She smiled, a pretty smile. 'He said that was because publishing and bookselling was run by men. Not any more. We're taking over the world, women. Wait till Hillary Clinton is President of the United States.'

'I know a few male chauvinists who'll leave for Mars that day. Including my husband.'

Wednesday morning Biddy called for her in a hire car. The children were still asleep and Leif came to the front door, in pyjamas and dressing-gown, to kiss her farewell. Then he looked past her and down at the car at the kerb. 'We should get one of those.'

She wasn't really interested in cars. She kissed his cheek, told him to have the girls at school by 8.30, to pick them up at 3.30 and she would be home by 5.30. 'I sound like a timetable.'

'Good luck,' he said, sincerely proud of her.

'We'll eat out,' she said and ran down to

the car.

She sank into its luxury, pressed Biddy's hand, then smiled at the driver as he was about to close the rear door on her. 'My husband is impressed by your car. What is it?'

'A Lexus 430. It's only a week old, I'm still getting used to it myself.'

They drove off and Marie settled back, enjoying the luxury. She had never been extravagant (Leif was the extravagant one, always saying tomorrow could look after itself), but all at once she wanted a car like this. She had the good taste not to ask the driver how much it had cost, but, unexpectedly, it was on her shopping list.

The Melbourne interviews were a success and she arrived home tired and happy. The girls hugged her as if she had been away on a world tour; they were not accustomed to their mum being away. For her part, she felt she had been away from them for a week.

'Where do you want to eat?'

'Pizza Hut!' Gourmets both.

'If they were older,' said Leif, 'we could take them Otto's or Lucio's. We could start with lobster bisque–'

'Tonight, sweetheart, you eat pizza and love it.'

Later, round a mouthful of cheese and

pastry, Leif said, 'I ran into Jack Hemming today. He said he and Liz were looking forward to Friday night, they hadn't seen the Delmonicos in months–'

'Oh, God!' Marie wiped cheese from her lips. 'I'd forgotten! I thought it was Friday week–'

Leif looked at her affectionately. 'Sweetheart, you'd better come back to earth.'

'Why?' said Brigid. 'Where's she been?'

'On cloud nine–' He was smiling at Marie and she loved him, wanted to reach across the table and grab him to her. But Pizza Hut was no love nest.

She was in a cocoon of success. Out in the real world the dollar, the economy and the stock market were all falling. The price of oil was gushing skywards and the housing boom was turning to smoke. On the far side of the real world, European unity was becoming a music-hall joke. Afghanistan and Iraq were dry quagmires of rock and sand and a six-foot-six, bearded wraith, who had been sought for four years, was still sending threatening messages to Washington. But she was still in her bubble. Pizza Hut had not recognized her tonight, but soon, soon...

'Mum,' said Rosie, 'what are you staring at?'

'I'm dreaming,' said Marie and took another bite of pizza.

Later, in bed, Leif said, 'When does the money start coming in?'

She wasn't irritated by the question; it was a practical one. She had once been careless of money; now she was counting it. 'Joe says September... Would you like a Lexus 630?'

'Four thirty.' He propped himself on an elbow. 'You seriously mean it?'

She nodded, seriously pleased at the look on his face; he was her one man, no matter how imperfect and annoying he could sometimes be. 'When the money comes in–'

'We could put our order in now. They probably don't have them waiting on the showroom floor–' He was like Brigid and Rosie at Christmas.

'No, let's wait till we see how big the cheques are going to be. In the meantime, what do I feed the Hemmings and Delmonicos Friday night?'

'Well, we could start with lobster bisque–'

'Touch me,' she said and drew him to her before he sent them bankrupt.

Dinner for the Hemmings and Delmonicos did not begin with lobster bisque but it did end with champagne, brought by both pairs of guests to celebrate their hostess' promised fame.

'I once read that Ernest Hemingway made no money at all from his first two books.' Jack Hemming, short and compact and with a lively face, was the doctor who had delivered Brigid and Rosie. 'Of course, he had a wife who had her own trust fund.'

'The best sort of wife,' said Leif, and smiled across the table at his own trust fund.

'He didn't write children's books.' Edith Hemming was also short and compact, with a composure to offset her husband's energy. 'He knew nothing about kids and he knew nothing about women. They were all idolized.'

'Isn't that what you women want?' asked Leif.

'I like escapism.' Gretel Delmonico had been an in-house model for a clothing manufacturer now out of business due to Asian competition. She was darkly attractive and twelve years younger than her husband. She looked at other men and commented on them to Marie and her friends. She had once innocently (though Marie doubted her innocence) commented on how attractive Leif was. 'I open the newspaper every morning and it's just bad news. Dreary.'

'My dad reckons the best period ever was the Fifties.' Larry Delmonico would have been good-looking if there had been less of him. There was too much of him to appreciate; you looked for the carnival mirror that was distorting him. He was a senior public servant with the Ministry of Health, a hive of bad news with hospital ward shutdowns, not enough doctors and nurses, finance deficits. 'Doris Day singing, no women's lib–'

Marie and Edith whacked him. 'Castrate him,' Edith told her husband. Then apologized to Gretel: 'Sorry. That would ruin things for you.' Then she threw up her hands: 'Why do they always have that to hold over us?'

'Do you mind?' said Leif, sure of himself as he was of the other two males. 'Can we get back to children's books? Have you read *Winnie the Pooh* lately?'

When the guests were leaving, Larry Delmonico said, 'How are things in the new set-up at Intra-Urban?'

'I'm getting used to it. Much less work.'

'Care to swap? At Health all we have is headaches.'

Leif smiled, patted Larry on the back. 'Enjoy them.'

He closed the front door, leaned against it, looked at Marie in the dining-room doorway. 'I'm glad I'm not Larry. As he said, nothing but headaches... Let's go to bed.'

'We've still got to clear everything–'

'Leave it till morning–'

'You take the girls to soccer tomorrow and I do the ironing. We clean up tonight.'

It was a conversation that was echoed all over Sydney. Dirty dishes are stubborn in their inertia.

They went to bed half an hour later too tired for love-making. Leif wrapped his arms round Marie, close as love could make them.

Saturday morning Leif took the girls to soccer while Marie did the ironing. At one point she paused, dreaming: did Joanne Rowling have a housekeeper to do the ironing? Did the Tolkien heirs have house help? Hemingway, she had read, had had four wives, so he had never had to worry about the ironing. Then she went back to Leif's shirts. Why did he always wear soft collars, where you had to be careful you didn't iron creases *into* the collars instead of *out* of them?

Leif's parents had retired to Cowra, 300 kilometres to the west, and he and Marie saw them only three or four times a year. But his mother called every Saturday at lunchtime, as she did today: 'I've just finished your book. It's not a good lesson for kids, do you think, robbing a bank? Have Brigid and Rosie read it?'

'Brigid has. She's out now casing a bank... Only joking, Maeve. Has Liam read it?'

'He thought it very funny. He never reads anything to improve himself.'

'How's the drought out your way?'

'Pretty grim. I'm glad we didn't buy a property.' They lived in the town and were comfortably fixed; Liam had owned two service stations and had got out when they were still saleable. 'Are the girls there?'

'They're not back from soccer yet–'

'I don't think girls should be playing football, they'll grow up – what's the word? You're the writer.'

'Hoydens?'

'That'll do. Well, tell them to call me. Liam sends his love and says don't spend all the money at once.'

Marie knew that was Maeve's advice, not Liam's. She hung up. She was learning that the world is full of literary critics.

Leif came home with the hoydens-in-the-making, the Misses Beckham. 'They both scored a goal. Rosie's was in her own goal, but she's claiming credit for it, anyway.'

Marie kissed her youngest. 'Congratulations, darling. Never let anyone put you down, not even referees. Now call Grandma Johnson and tell her all about it.' She straightened up, looked at Leif. 'Your mum's a literary critic now.'

'It's the Irish in her,' said Leif with a grin. 'What's for lunch?'

Wednesday evening Marie and Leif were going to a function at Parliament House. Louise came straight from work to babysit her favourite, her only, nieces. They greeted her with screams of delight, as if she were Angelina Jolie come to adopt them. She had brought a cheap bottle of perfume and she sprayed them with it and they swanned around in a haze of Woolworths No. 5.

'We shan't be late,' said Marie. 'It's just drinks and dry biscuits. The government is celebrating ten years in office. Billy Eustace still can't spend money.' Eustace was the State Premier, a politician who had arrived in the position by accident and, to everyone's surprise, including his own, had survived. 'Leif and the other PR men have to gladhand the press. The wives and I will just be wallpaper.'

'Ain't it the way?' said Louise, and the two sisters kissed each other while Leif looked on tolerantly.

An hour later Marie was part of the wallpaper in the big reception room, listening to the party crackers of cocktail chatter:

'Darling, if she had only one leg she'd still have the world at her foot. That's Sydney—'

'He thinks anonymity is an ambition and he's almost there—'

'He says he's in the sunset of his career, but when the sun goes down, so will he—'

Then Billy Eustace recognized her. His eagle eye, like all politicians', had been trained to recognize a voter; the human side of him had been trained to recognize a pretty woman, who is always more interesting than a mere voter. He was bald and thin and had once been tentative, but assurance had been thrust upon him by his minders and now he occasionally sounded like a leader. He wore starched button-down collars so he was not entirely relaxed, at least sartorially. He had a pleasant smile, one of the few attributes he didn't have to work on.

'I read your book to my grandkids. But I wondered if it was meant for them? It's

174

meant to be a satire on politics, am I right?'

'Partly,' said Marie, diplomatically but not satirically. She was waiting for St Mary's Cathedral to comment on the religious significance of it and compare Barney Guinness to St Paul.

'I'm looking for someone to write my autobiography.' He looked at her hopefully.

'The field's crowded at the moment,' she said, dodging the invitation. 'Twenty-year-old sports stars are writing their life stories. I hear a 12-year-old skateboarder has got his autobiography coming out for Christmas.'

Then she was saved by one of the Premier's minders coming up to say the Paraguayan consul-general had arrived and Billy Eustace went off to greet a guest more important than a writer of satirical children's books. Marie accepted a consoling drink from a passing waiter and turned to face Dinah Camplin.

'What a nice surprise!'

Dinah smiled. She wore an apple-green dress that obviously was not office wear; it showed cleavage deep enough to have been a filing cabinet. 'Three or four of us were dragooned into coming. We're supposed to butter-up the unattached males. There are hordes of them.'

'We have our uses,' said Marie. 'What lovely earrings!'

'They were my great-grandmother's, they've been handed down.' Dinah fingered one of them. 'They are one of the zodiac signs. Virgo.'

'Virgin?' It sounded like a swear-word in this gathering.

'It was an old family tradition. Well, up to puberty. How are Brigid and Rosie?'

'A long way from puberty, thank God. How are things in the new set-up? Are you working with my husband?'

'Not directly. It's quite a comedown from the old ministry set-up, but I've got used to it. It's less impersonal, you feel you're dealing with people, not just files.'

Then Leif came up, smiling, and said pleasantly, 'What are you two nattering about?'

'Virginity,' said Marie.

'Remembering it,' said Dinah, virginally.

'You talk about a subject like that in Parliament House? That's obscene.'

'Don't worry, sweetheart,' said Marie. 'We shan't spread the word. Will we, Dinah?'

'Mum's the word,' said Dinah, then smiled at them both and melted away, earrings dangling like beckoning signs, to butter-up some more unattached males.

Marie looked after her. 'Is she efficient, good to work with?'

'I hardly see her. I've got my own helpers.'

Dinah, across the room, was being assailed by three unattached males, including the Paraguayan consul-general, trying to attach themselves to her like limpet fish. 'She can handle men.'

'So can you. At least, this one.' He put his arm round her.

'And don't forget it,' she said and kissed his cheek as the Premier passed by, nodding approvingly at the demonstration of marital bliss.

Chapter Ten

1

Leif was enjoying Marie's success; he wasn't in the least envious. As he explained to Dinah, in bed in her flat, 'She's not letting it go to her head–'

'Do we have to talk about her?' said Dinah, but then, womanly, as he thought, went on, 'What's she going to do with all the money she's going to make?'

'It's still promises, promises.' He didn't know why he had got into a discussion about his wife with another woman, in the other woman's bed. 'She's not spending the money yet.'

'Will she let you spend any of it?'

He twisted his head on the pillow. 'Why?'

'We could find an excuse to go away for a week. New Zealand or Fiji.'

She was becoming too possessive. He had rung Marie this afternoon to say he had to work back and would be late. He had made up his mind that this would be his farewell tryst, a word he liked, with Dinah. So far he hadn't mentioned it, struck dumb by sex; farewell is the last thought in mind when the loins are pumping away like a threshing machine. He sat up, his back to her and stared at the bedroom wall. Then, only half-turning, he said, 'We're finished, Dinah. It's over.'

She reacted as he had expected; she was quick to anger. She jumped out of bed, clenched her fists as if about to hit him. 'You bastard! You think you can dump me like that?'

He stood up, faced her. He was surprised at how detached he was, that he saw them both, him and her, as if standing off from them. There is nothing more ridiculous than two naked people standing off arguing with each other. Primeval it may be, but it was still ridiculous. His still semi-stiff penis wobbled like a misplaced, remonstrating finger.

'I'm not dumping you – for Crissake, Dinah, it could never go on and on! I'm happily married–' Even in his own ears that sounded a laughable argument.

'Happily married – but you still want your piece on the side! What's the matter – doesn't she know how to satisfy you like I do?'

He felt a sudden surge of anger, wanted to hit her. Somehow he managed to control himself, turned and headed for the bathroom.

'Where are you going?' she demanded.

'Have a shower, then I'll be gone–'

'No you don't! Go home to your own fucking bathroom–' Then she seemed to become aware that she was still naked; she looked around, grabbed a robe and struggled into it. He was aware that there was anger in her, but till now he had never seen it. 'Get out! Get your things and get out!'

Then she almost raced out of the bedroom. He stood for a moment, still naked, then he began to dress. He was all thumbs as he tried to do up buttons; the zipper on his fly stuck, as if to mock him. He had had half a dozen affairs, but none of the women had acted like Dinah. They had not been possessive, they had been *civilized*, another of his favourite words. At last he was ready to go. He went into the bathroom, wet a tissue and wiped the lipstick from his face.

He looked at himself in the mirror, saw the shame he suddenly felt; not at what he had just done to Dinah, but at what he had been doing to Marie. Conscience, like CityRail, is often a late arrival.

He went out into the living room, heading for the front door. There he paused, looked back at her standing in the kitchen doorway, not languid but threatening.

They stared at each other, then he closed the door on her, went down the small hall-way hoping no one had heard their row. He had come here without ever having been seen by her three neighbours; they had never come in together, he always following her after five minutes. He went down the hill to his car, parked as always in the main road; a bitter wind came up from the south, making his eyes water like tears. He got into the car, sat for a long moment staring at the cemetery, the headstones cold as up-ended ice-floes in the winter moonlight. A large scrap of paper blew amongst the graves, like a soul that had wandered and was lost. Then he started up the car, swung it round and headed for home.

He was halfway there, in strange territory, when he suddenly got the shakes. He slowed the car, pulled over to the kerb and stopped. Then saw the police car pulling up behind him, its red and blue lights slowly flashing like a sardonic smile. Two officers got out of the car and came towards him.

He lowered the side window, feeling the

cold air hit him, and said, 'Something wrong, officer?'

'You looked unsteady, sir. Will you blow into this?' He was a young constable, polite as schoolboys used to be. He handed Leif the register, Leif blew into it, handed it back to the officer, who checked it. 'You are clear, sir.'

'I haven't had a drink all night. I had – I had a fit of sneezing, that was why I pulled up.'

'Good judgement, sir. Have a nice night.'

The two officers looked at each other as if they had heard a score of excuses for erratic driving and went back to their own car. Leif drove on, feeling as if he had just escaped drowning in a flooded river.

Marie was in bed reading a Kerry Greenwood crime novel. She put it down and looked at him. 'You look beat–'

'I am.' He kissed her, then undressed and headed for the bathroom. 'I think I may be getting the 'flu. I'll have a shower, warm up and come to bed.'

Five minutes later he came out of the bathroom, pulled on his pyjama pants and coat, which he rarely wore, and climbed into bed. Marie turned to him, reached for him.

'Not tonight, Josephine,' he said, managing to smile as he said it.

'I called you at the office – where were you?'

'I was there. It must've been when I went for some coffee. I'm bushed, love. Really.'

She kissed him tenderly and he turned over on his side, facing her. *What a bloody fool I am.* Conscience was a weight in his crotch, like a third ball, a leaden one. Philandering was over, he was determined about that.

2

The Minister for Local Government, the sworn enemy of municipal councils, had had a convenient prostate operation. The Premier, another on the outer with councils, had had a convenient engagement elsewhere. And so Steven Perkins, now a general dogsbody, had been drafted to open the annual conference of municipal councils.

Leif was working on the speech with Jill Bessemer. She was an attractive woman, slightly overweight and unworried about it, and amiable with those she worked with. She had begun her working life as an 18-year-old cadet on a morning newspaper and now, twenty-two years later wore cynicism as a girdle. She could write a twenty-minute speech for a minister that, on analysis, said nothing, which was what the minister had wanted. She defended the poor and the indefensible (and that was just among the MPs) and wrote power speeches for ministers who thought theirs was the power. Banks and insurance companies, institutions lately in need of a polish, enticed her with huge offers, but she always shook her head. Politics was her life, though she would never run for office.

'Lies,' she said now, sitting across from Leif in his office, 'are the *lingua franca* of today–'

'And we're so fluent in it,' said Leif.

'–but we must give our boy something that sounds like the truth, the whole truth and nothing but the truth. And I don't think there's any point in adding "So help me, God", because I think God has just given up in disgust.'

'Why can't we give him that?' said Leif. 'The truth, the whole truth and nothing but the truth.'

'Wash your mouth out,' said Jill. 'That's heresy. The walls would come tumbling down.'

Then Dinah appeared in the office doorway, not languidly but almost demurely. 'Mr Johnson, may I – oh, I'm sorry, I'll come back later–'

'No,' said Leif, wanting the protection of Jill's company. 'What is it?'

'I'm leaving, I've been offered another job. As a receptionist at–' She named one of the leading five-star hotels. 'I'd like a reference.'

'No trouble, Dinah.' He was distant but courteous. 'I'll see you have it by lunchtime.'

'Thank you. And excuse me for interrupting–' She turned and went away, the swing of her arse as demure as that of a young girl who had just taken her first Communion.

'She'll make a good receptionist,' said Jill. 'On her feet or on her back. Has she ever made a pass at you?'

'Not that I've noticed.' He had looked at Dinah this morning and been surprised he could do it objectively. He had been calm, another surprise. His new-found morality was not a hairshirt, after all. 'Has she got that reputation?'

'No, that's just observation on my part. She'd be user-friendly. Now where were we in our search for the truth, the whole truth and nothing but the truth?'

'We'd decided to leave God out of it.'

'He'd be glad to hear it.'

They finished the speech, a balloon filled with the hot air of platitudes, and Jill departed. Leif looked at the papers on his desk, then decided to get Dinah's reference out of the way. It took three drafts to keep it impersonal as well as personal. At midday she was back, knocking on his door like a junior clerk.

'Am I too soon?'

'No, come in.' He remained seated, a boss. He handed her the reference: 'I've kept it handwritten. Makes it more personal, as if we've had close association.'

That was a blunder and she smiled at it. 'May I sit down?' He nodded and she arranged herself on the chair in front of his desk. She looked a little stilted but it was a parody; she would be languid in her coffin. 'Leif, you can relax. You are a bastard, an absolute shit, but it's over. If we had been French and in Paris, I could've been your *cinq à sept* mistress and everything would've been fine.'

'You've overlooked one thing. My wife isn't French.'

'True. A pity. You know, while I was with you, I never gave her a thought. Did you?' She stood up. 'Thanks for the reference. I

186

can't give you one, except how good in bed you are. Remember me to Brigid and Rosie.'

She left and this time the swing of her arse was like a thumb to the nose. For a moment he had a sexual memory, then he shook his head and cursed himself. He spent the rest of the day re-shuffling himself. He would be a faithful husband, a devoted father, a paragon. It was, of course, another bubble of platitude. But self-delusion has its uses.

He went home, kissed and hugged Brigid and Rosie as if he had just fathered them. Then he went into the kitchen, where Marie was putting dinner on the plates, and hugged and kissed her, as if embarking on a second honeymoon.

She, putting first things first, said, 'Watch it, or the gravy's going to finish up on the floor. You've had a good day, I take it?'

'Well, up to a point–' He retreated, not wanting to be too obvious in his conversion. 'I'm getting used to the new set-up. There's much less pressure.' Indeed there was, with Dinah gone. 'You had a good day?'

'The usual. Taking the girls to school, doing the housework, darning your socks–'

He grinned, loving her for her down-to-earth attitude.

'Nothing else?'

'Well, yes–' They were in the dining room, settling down at the table.

'Oh, God,' said Brigid, looking at her plate. 'Broccoli again!'

'Shut up and eat up... Joe phoned me. We got two more foreign offers today.'

'Great!' He was really pleased for her. 'But...'

'Mum,' said Rosie, 'do I have to eat the broccoli?'

'Shut up and eat up... But what?'

'Do you want to go on writing?' He chewed on a portion of pork sausage; she knew he liked them and bought them specially for him. 'You haven't been near the computer since you finished the Barney book.'

'My mind's been full of other things–' She picked at her food.

'You're not eating *your* broccoli,' said Brigid.

Marie ate a mouthful. 'My mind's not working, sweetheart. I mean, coming up with an idea for another book. I've read that it happens – there's an author who took seven years to write her second book... My editor wants me to do another one with Barney and his mates, but my mind's just a blank. I guess it's the distraction of all these offers coming in–'

'Some distraction,' said Leif and leaned across and kissed her.

'Urk!' said Brigid.

'What are you urking at? Me kissing Mum?'

'No, the broccoli–'

They finished dinner, Marie took the dishes into the kitchen and he took the girls to their shower. He felt the sudden comfort of domesticity, as if he had just discovered it. He put the girls to bed, hugged them, felt another comfort, that of being a father, and then went out to the living room, all at once wanting a few moments alone.

Suddenly, as if wanting to remember them before erasing them forever from his memory, he thought of girls he had known, some of them, apart from Dinah, since his marriage. They were adventures (who was he kidding?) that should never have begun; but he wondered how many men he knew had gone the same route (wrong word). Men don't like to think of themselves as the only sinner. For a moment he thought of Louise, but the stab of shame was too much.

'What are you thinking about?' Marie came into the room, dropped into her favourite chair. 'You look – troubled?'

'Do I?' He was surprised; it hadn't

occurred to him that his thoughts might have come to the surface. 'I – I wasn't thinking about anything. Don't you feel sometimes it's a relief to be blank-minded?'

'I'm often like that, but it's no relief. It's called writer's block, something I never thought I'd suffer from. It's so – so pretentious-sounding.'

'Most of the writers who are interviewed sound pretentious. But so does PR writing, sometimes. And advertising copywriting.' He looked at her, loving her, Dinah and all the other women suddenly gone, and mouthed a kiss at her. 'I'm ready for early bed, what about you?'

'Not yet, not if what you have in mind... The girls aren't asleep yet.'

Family, occasionally, is a wet blanket.

Chapter Eleven

1

Marie woke Friday morning with her period, three days early, which always made her bad-tempered. Her nipples were sore, as they often were when she came early, and when Leif, half-awake, turned towards her and put his hand on her breast she slapped it away. 'Keep it to yourself!'

He blinked awake. 'Why, what's the matter?'

'I've got my period–'

He frowned. 'You're early, aren't you?'

'Yes! What do you do, keep a calendar on me?'

He was wide awake now. 'No, I don't! For Crissake – I'm not the sort of husband who thinks his wife shouldn't have her period–'

'Sorry–'

She slid out of bed, went into the bathroom and shut the door. She leaned on the washbasin, looking at herself in the mirror. The bad temper had started only over the last couple of months; it was as if the blood itself became angry. Why was it that only women had this inconvenience? God, a male, wouldn't you know it, had played this trick on them. When, if, she got to heaven she would have a word or two with Him... She smiled at herself in the mirror, but it was only a grimace. Then she began to look for tampons and suddenly remembered she had forgotten to buy them this week. *Damn!* She looked for a facecloth...

At breakfast Brigid said, 'Why's Mum in a bad mood?'

'She's not feeling well,' said Leif.

'Jade says her mum's always in a bad mood,' said Rosie.

'Do you kids sit around all day talking about your mums?' snapped Marie.

'Yes. And our dads.'

'Drink your orange juice!'

'I think I must get along to the school some day,' said Leif. 'Hear what they have to say about the other dads.'

'You might get a surprise or two,' said Marie.

When he was leaving Leif kissed her gently on the cheek. 'Take it easy, sweetheart. I do sympathize—'

'I know,' she said and kissed him in return.

'Did you leave that suit out for me to take to the cleaners?'

'It's on the bed.' He kissed her again and was gone.

She was disorganized, as she often was when she had her period. She was running late. She bundled the girls into the back of the car, buckled their seatbelts, fumbling with the locks. She threw the dry-cleaning into the front seat beside her. She fumbled with the ignition key and heard Brigid, behind her, say to Rosie, 'Hang on tight, we're gunna go fast!'

Marie looked in the driving mirror at the two of them, tried for calm, smiled at them, all at once glad she had them.

'Pull your head in, sister–'

The two girls smiled at her, then shrank their heads into their shoulders.

She dropped them off at the school, kissed and hugged them as if she had been in an argument with them, spoke to a couple of the other mothers, waved to a teacher and went back to her car. She got in, sat for a few moments, looking at Brigid and Rosie gossiping with some of their friends, and, as happened so often, realized how lucky she was.

Then she started up the car, drove on to

the shopping centre and the dry-cleaning shop. She pulled into the parking lot, switched off the engine, then picked up the skirt and cardigan which she had brought with Leif's suit. There was nothing in the cardigan's pockets, no old tissues, no earrings taken off and put there and forgotten. Then she picked up Leif's suit.

It was a Hugo Boss; he had three of them. This navy blue one was her favourite; he always looked so smart in it, a clothes-stallion, not a clothes-horse. She began to go through the pockets; he never seemed to do that himself. A soiled handkerchief in a trouser pocket, some loose change. Then she went through the jacket pockets. Nothing in the left-hand side pocket, but something in the right-hand pocket. She took it out and recognized it at once: one of Dinah Camplin's zodiac earrings. Marie frowned, mind still a little blank. She turned the earring over in the palm of her hand, trying to shut her mind against the suspicion creeping into it. Almost automatically, still looking at the earring in one hand, she put her other hand into the jacket's inside pocket. And drew out a folded sheet of paper, a small page from a pocket diary. On it was a scrawled telephone number, not a mobile number, with the letter D beside it.

Suddenly she felt sick, sicker than when she had woken earlier this morning. The bad temper flared up, she felt ready to burst. *Oh, you bastard!* Once or twice she had suspected him of having an affair, but she had never questioned him; she had treasured what they had and she had not wanted to crumble it with suspicion. But now...

She grabbed the clothes, got out of the car, stumbling as if her eyes weren't working properly, locked the car, fumbling with the remote on the key. She stood for a moment, waiting to get strength back into her legs, hardly aware of the cold wind turning her hair into a madwoman's wig. Then, legs responding, she almost raced across the parking lot to the dry-cleaning shop, as if the Hugo Boss suit, *his* suit, had to be thrown away before it contaminated her.

'Why, Mrs Johnson!' Mrs Tiller, the owner of the shop, was a big bundle of giggles and laughter, as if it was her job to keep the whole world in good humour. Marie would tell her some of the milder jokes Leif brought home from the office and she would respond with a roar of laughter that would have done credit to a thousand throats.

'My boy, Redwood, is reading your book–'

195

She gurgled, as if at the thought. 'Hasn't read a book, ever–'

Redwood? Where did they get these names? 'Is he liking it?'

'Loving it! Are you going to be the new Harry Potter?'

'That would need a sex change and I'm not ready for that yet–'

She went out of the shop on another surfing gale of laughter. She went back to her car, as if it were a refuge, got in and sat looking at the earring and the slip of paper again. There was the Friday shopping to do, but her mind was a blank list there. Then she gritted her teeth, as if about to climb a rope up a cliff, put the slip of paper and the earring in the pocket of her coat, got out of the car and went into the supermarket. Routine had to be kept; she remembered her mother had, long ago, taught her that.

The supermarket, environmentally conscious, supplied large brown-paper bags instead of plastic bags. Her mood was not helped when, lifting a bag out of the shopping trolley to put it in the car, the bag broke and the contents spilled onto the ground. She was on the verge of tears when she finally got into the car. She sat for a while, then looked at herself in the driving mirror. The Mad Woman of Chaillot, The Wreck of the Hesperus; take your pick. She ran a comb through her hair, wiped her eyes, then drove home carefully, as if not quite sure of her reaction to traffic hazards.

She had brought in the last of the groceries, dumped them on the kitchen table, when her mobile rang. It was Leif: 'I'm going to be late tonight, sweetheart. Don't wait dinner for me–'

'Why, what's the sudden call tonight?' Her voice, she knew, was sharp with suspicion.

'The boss is on an emergency committee, about security. What happened in London yesterday has got everyone wondering what *we* should do. It's not panic stations, but it's going to be heads down and arses up for a day or two. How are you feeling?'

'Awful,' she said and clicked off her mobile.

A moment or two, then the mobile rang again. She stared at it, but didn't pick it up. Then it was silent, no message on it. And she looked at her hands and saw that they were shaking.

She put away the groceries, then went into the main bedroom and lay on the still unmade bed. She felt sick, then she began to weep. She lay, miserable and self-pitying, for almost an hour; it was out of character for her, but she didn't realize it. At last she got up, stripped off and went into the bathroom and showered. She stood under the water, bugger the restrictions, for fifteen minutes, as if everything, doubt, suspicion, could be washed away. She got out of the shower-stall, dried herself, replaced the facecloth with a tampon she had bought, went back into the bedroom and put on a skirt and jumper, dressing carefully, taking her time, as if putting off something that she didn't want to do.

Then she went out to the handset in the hallway and rang the Office of Intra-Urban Development. 'Could you put me through to Dinah Camplin, please?'

'I'm sorry, Miz Camplin is no longer with us. She left yesterday–'

Marie hung up and only then did it strike her: she had been going to go to town, to the government office, and to confront Dinah Camplin with the earring and the home phone number.

Jesus! She thought and almost hit herself. *How stupid could I be? Fronting up to her in her workplace, with everyone looking on!*

But her mood and her discomfort did not improve during the day. The hours seemed to stretch and she was glad when the time came to pick up the girls at school. She bundled them into the car, tried hard not to snap at them. She looked at them as she turned in the front seat to make sure their seatbelts were buckled. *I can't lose you,* she thought. And wondered if Leif thought about them when he went to bed with that whore.

She cooked dinner for them and herself; tried to fit into the routine of a normal day. But the effort wore her out and, when the girls were in bed, she went back into the kitchen, sat down at the table and then became aware of her mobile, lying on the table like a temptation. She couldn't resist it.

She punched in Leif's direct office number. It rang and rang and she was about to dump it back on the table when a woman's voice said, 'Mr Johnson's office–'

'This is Mrs Johnson. Is my husband there?'

'No, Mrs Johnson. He left about an hour ago–'

'Thank you,' said Marie, stiffly polite, and clicked off the mobile. She held it, looking at it as if it were some sort of traitor's instrument. Then she slammed it down on the table.

And Brigid at the kitchen door said, 'What's up, Mum?'

Marie looked at her, dim through tears. 'I'm just not well, darling. Women sometimes get like this.'

Brigid moved to her, put her arms round her neck. 'I don't like it when you're not happy.'

'I'm happy, darling.' Somehow she managed a smile. 'You can feel unwell and still be happy.'

'I dunno I wanna grow up–' She was now sitting on Marie's lap. 'Ginny Lopez says her mother cries all the time.'

Marie did not know Ginny Lopez's mother. 'Maybe she has troubles. I don't cry all the time, do I?'

'No-o. But I like it better when you're laughing.'

'I'll practise,' she said and gave an imitation of a laugh. 'There, how's that? Now go back to bed – and don't wake Rosie.'

Brigid slid off her lap and went back to bed. Marie sat there in the kitchen for another half-hour, debating whether to wait up for Leif. Had he gone to meet Dinah Camplin somewhere, maybe dinner together; or somewhere else, where there was a bed. She was torturing herself, she knew that, but she was jealous. From her university studies she remembered something by that old misogynist, Euripides: *Jealousy is inborn in women's hearts*. Maybe he was right, but why did a man have to say it? Men were always telling women what was wrong with them... Leif did it, every man she had ever known had done it.

She picked up the mobile again, took out the slip of paper she had carried with her all day, self-torture. She looked at the number, then punched it into her mobile. The number rang and rang, then a voice said, languid (she thought) as a whore's: 'This is Dinah. I'm not available at the moment, but if you leave your name and number–'

Marie clicked off the mobile, dropped it back on the table. *I'm not available at the moment*... Like a hooker who would be free as soon as she got rid of her current client– 'Oh, come on!' Marie snapped at herself. But she felt no better.

She went to bed, but couldn't sleep. She was still awake when Leif came in at 11 o'clock. 'You awake?'

'Yes. Don't turn on the light–' As if there was some sort of refuge in the dark. 'How did your meeting go?'

'Round and round in circles. We're novices

at this game, we're still learning how to *spell* terrorism.' He was getting undressed by the light from the bathroom. 'How are the girls?'

'Fine.' She was lying on her back, looking at his moving silhouette. Would he go into the bathroom, wash that whore off himself? 'I called your office. You weren't there.'

'We'd gone out for something to eat. Why didn't you call me on my mobile?'

'I didn't want to disturb you.' *Not if you were in bed with her.*

He went into the bathroom, relieved himself, cleaned his teeth; did nothing more. He switched off the bathroom light, got into bed, wearing only his pyjama pants. 'How are you feeling?'

'Lousy,' she said and turned away from him. 'Don't touch me. Just go to sleep.'

He didn't press her, said solicitously, 'You'll feel better in the morning.'

Chapter Twelve

1

Joe was conducting a conference between Mr and Mrs Pincole, which he had called against the wishes of Mr Pincole. Husband and wife sat apart, like strangers at an employment office. Mrs Pincole was black-haired, well-dressed and attractive, but very thin, as if nymphomania worked better than a Jenny Craig diet. She was nervous and fidgety, while her husband sat like a rock in his chair. Joe, shrugging mentally at the task ahead, began:

'Mrs Pincole, Harold agreed to this meeting–'

'Only under pressure,' said Harold.

'I was so glad he did. I've lost so much weight worrying–'

So it was worry or anguish of conscience, not nymphomania. Weight Watchers and Jenny Craig would be glad to hear that. 'I understand you want a reconciliation–'

'No way,' said Pincole, who looked as if he

had put *on* weight since the separation.

Joe waved a restrained hand. 'Let me get through this, Harold...' He turned over the paper he held. 'This confession you've signed on the back of your dog's registration licence–'

'That's the terrible part–' She choked back a sob, blew her nose. 'I never dreamed Francoise's name would be dragged into a divorce–'

Joe looked blank, turned to Harold, who said, 'Our French poodle. I wasn't thinking when I grabbed that piece of paper – I was so bloody angry–'

'Harold, sweetheart–' There was no doubt she loved her husband. Joe suddenly felt sorry for her, was on her side. 'Every time I used to close my eyes and pretend it was you–'

Harold snorted like a bull that had been wounded.

'–I never thought of myself as being unfaithful – it was just I couldn't help myself, you know how much we both love sex–'

Joe coughed. 'Would you like me to leave the room?'

'No, stay where you are,' said Harold as if afraid to be left alone with this nympho-maniac.

'I only went to the best bars, you know, fourteen dollars for a cocktail–'

'Jesus!' said Harold. 'On my money!'

'Harold, I always took it out of housekeeping–'

Harold looked at Joe. 'I don't want to get too personal ... but you're divorced, aren't you? How did you handle it?'

'No fuss, Harold. We were just – just incompatible, no adultery. I think you two *are* compatible – except for the adultery.' *I'm glad no court is listening to this.* 'Go away and give some more thought to it. We've still got a fortnight–'

'If we go to court,' said Mrs Pincole, 'will you show that paper?'

'No, Mrs Pincole. We'll keep Francoise's name out of it.'

Five minutes later Joe was alone. He blew out, as if exhausted, and looked up as Edith came into his office. It was a relief to see someone as solid and down-to-earth as Edith.

'How did Mr Pincole and the sexpot go?'

'I think – I hope – there may be a reconciliation. Did she throw him to the floor when they got outside?'

'Not that I noticed.'

'If he gave up the sea and found a shore

job, say in a lighthouse–' Where the Pincoles could make love all day while the light was out.

'Maybe they could open a sex shop?'

'You're too cynical, Edith. What's new?'

Edith laid some papers on his desk. 'Assault and battery. This girl beat up her boyfriend – he was in hospital for two weeks–'

'*She* bashed *him?* What are you women coming to?' Then he looked again at the notice. 'Wait a minute – I'm defending the girl and not pleading for the bloke?'

Edith just smirked and left the room.

Joe sank back in his chair, all at once decided he didn't want an empty evening ahead of him. He ran over in his mind possible dinner partners: Lisa, Kylie, Sharon. Sharon? No, he had decided she was too close to home. Prospective girlfriends should be kept at a distance, like in-laws and process servers. He found himself dialling Louise at work:

'Would you care for dinner tonight?'

'Funny you should ask. Yes. Where?'

'I'll pick you up–'

'No, I'll meet you wherever it is–'

'How about Machiavelli, seven o'clock?'

He hung up, wondering if he had chosen the right dinner partner. He was still in love with Louise and almost loved her again; which is a different thing. Working amongst broken marriages, he was cautious of re-commitment. And he was unsure of Louise herself.

He put on the second new suit he had bought; he would never become fashion-conscious, but he was no longer a scarecrow. Edith and Shanyne had gone out and bought him a Hermes tie and presented him with the bill; he had threatened to sack them on the spot. But he put on the tie now and admitted it looked better than the nylon ones he usually wore. During their marriage Louise had often complained about his wardrobe, but he had resisted her influence. He wondered why he now allowed himself to be dressed by his two secretaries. He must be getting soft.

He was waiting for her at Machiavelli when she arrived. She was not a woman who made *entrances;* but she always at-tracted attention. She came in, wrapped in a fawn woollen coat, cream scarf round her throat and draped over one shoulder, and four businessmen at a table by the door looked up from their wheeling-and-dealing to stare at her admiringly. She floated by them, came to Joe, kissed him as he stood up. He looked past her at the four business-men: *Beat that for wheeling-and-dealing.* Possession, even if slippery, goes to a man's head.

She slid out of her coat, unwound the scarf. He said, 'Women always look more dramatic in winter. It must be the scarves.'

'I'd look even more dramatic in sable.'

'I'm an animal rights man. You look pretty good.'

'You overdo the flattery, Joe. When you called I'd already decided on a going-over. I'd booked into a beauty salon and they gave me a body massage, then the owner gave me a facial. Beauty is in the eye of the beautician – you learn that on the beauty counter.'

'Okay,' he said with a grin. 'You're beautiful.'

'So are you – in a homely sort of way.' She looked around the restaurant, which at this hour was only half full. 'I've heard of this place, but I've never been here.'

'Marie's publisher introduced me to it. At lunchtime it's the Sydney equivalent of Renaissance Florence. I was looking for those velvet berets those guys used to wear.'

'It would suit you.' She had sat down, arranging herself, he noted, remembering, with natural grace. She wore a black trouser suit and a cream silk blouse. 'How's business?'

'Let's order first.' He turned to the waiter hovering by: 'The lady's middle name is Machiavelli. What can you recommend?'

The waiter smiled at Louise: 'Signorina, will you leave it to me?'

'Why not? But first I'd like a glass of champagne. That's the Madame du Barry in me.'

The waiter smiled as if his night had been made and went away. Joe looked at Louise with admiration, glad now that he had not phoned any of the other women on his list.

'How's business?' Louise repeated.

'More than I can handle. How am I treating it?' He hesitated, shook his head. Sometimes he became depressed at human behaviour; man's inhumanity to man (and woman) never seemed to improve. Politicians spoke of the world threat of terrorism, but there was one-on-one terrorism every day of the week. 'I was the public defender of a 19-year-old kid, a druggie. He beat up an old man and stole his wallet. I was prepared to give the kid the back of my hand – till I met him. He was cut-up, in tears at what he had done to the old guy. Then I met the parents and the older brother, none of whom put up a penny for his defence. Nor would they go into the box and speak for him. Straight-as-a-die Christians who'd treated the kid as a loser all his life. Some are like that, they are born losers. He got twelve months and he'll come out and go back to drugs and one day he'll be dead in a gutter from an overdose. And then the family will give him a Christian burial and feel they've done their duty.'

She reached across and touched his hand. 'You should've been a social worker, Joe.'

He smiled his small smile. 'Sometimes I am... Our girl Marie is still in the money. I drew up another two contracts for her yesterday, large print and audio. I just hope she and Leif can cope with the difference it's going to make to their lives.'

'She'll cope. I hope it's roses all the way for her from now on. She has never had to struggle, but I know how much she's wanted to be a writer. She tried adult novels, but they never seemed to get anywhere, all she got was rejection slips. I read one of her manuscripts once, about seven or eight years ago, and it was bloody awful. Everyone in it was – idealized, I think is the word I want. It was like eating a tin full of candied honey–'

'You should've been a literary critic–'

'I told her to forget the whole idea. It wasn't a sisterly thing to do and she sulked for a while. Then she started on those kids' books. And now... How's Leif taking it? All this money coming in?'

'I dunno. He seems genuinely proud of her – I don't think he's in the least jealous. I always thought that PR men and journalists had a book in a bottom drawer, but Leif doesn't.'

Louise's champagne arrived, and Joe's gin-and-tonic. The waiter said, 'The head chef is out of his mind at honouring Signorina Machiavelli. But if I may be so personal, you don't look Machiavellian.'

'What woman does?' said Joe.

The waiter nodded, as if he had been a victim, and went away. Joe raised his glass to Louise: 'Here's to your beautician.'

The dinner would have had the Borgias applauding and Joe and Louise left happy and replete. The four businessmen, still wheeling-and-dealing, paused again to admire Louise. Joe swept by them with all the arrogance of Cesare Borgia, cardinal's hat and all.

His car was parked at a nearby parking station and they walked down through the cold, windless night, with Louise clinging to his arm for warmth. For the moment they were a happy couple, if not married. A star fell across the sky, but neither of them saw it and a wish went unfulfilled.

'I'm not a winter girl,' said Louise.

'I remember,' said Joe. 'You wore thicker nightgowns than my grandmother.'

'When did you sleep with your grandmother?' The champagne and the following wine with dinner were having their effect.

He laughed, feeling better than he had in weeks, and opened the car door for her. 'Get in, Madame du Barry.'

They drove home in a mutual warmth that was familiar, a memory of other nights. They said little, as if nothing needed to be said; as if they were married. When they drew up outside her block of flats, Joe switched off the engine, turned and looked at her. She returned his gaze; the silence was eloquent. Then he leaned across, put a hand behind her head and drew her to him. There was no resistance; she opened her mouth under his. It was like old times.

She leaned back from him, smiling slightly. 'I think *you* are Machiavelli.'

He said nothing, one hand still behind her head, the other on her breast inside her topcoat.

Then she said, 'Come on up–'

2

Joe woke at 2 o'clock, lay for a moment getting his bearings. He had never slept in this bed and the surroundings were unfamiliar to him. Then he became aware of Louise beside him. He slid out of bed, careful not to disturb her. She stirred, but didn't waken, drugged by the wine and sex.

He picked up his clothes and, careful not to bump into anything, made his way out to the kitchen. There he closed the door and switched on the light. He dressed, rinsed his face under the kitchen tap, dried it with his handkerchief. Then he looked around for a scribble pad, found one. He paused, his pen in hand, then he wrote: *If you have regrets, I don't want to be here to see them. I'll call you.*

Then he let himself out of the flat, went down to his car and drove home. The night had turned out as he had hoped; even better. But he was still uncertain, on a shore of shifting sands. He had always lived on the cautious side of hope. Which had been one of his smaller faults that had annoyed Louise; and he smiled at the thought as he drove home through the shank of the night. When he went to bed, to his own bed big enough for three (were king-sized beds designed for a *ménage-à-trois?*), he was still not sure what tomorrow (or today) would bring. He fell into a dreamless sleep, a clean slate.

He didn't call Louise first thing in the morning, before she went to work. He had learned enough about women to know that it didn't pay to rush them; Eve, he was sure, had taken her time before saying Yes to Adam. He remembered the old joke about Adam coming back to God and asking, 'What's a headache?' He noted that she did not call him.

His had been a cautious life, always one step behind the leaders of the pack. He had never fought bulls, ridden a picador's horse. He had played cricket at school and university, the all-rounder who batted Number 7, was third-change bowler. In winter he had played soccer, to please his father, who still revered Real Madrid and blessed himself when the name di Stefano was uttered. He had graduated middle of his class, worked for a while with a major firm of solicitors, then branched out on his own and done better than he, or his lecturers, would have expected. He was an also-ran who, against expectations, including his own, always got a place but was never first past the post. His biggest success had been in winning Louise, but that had gone awry and he wasn't sure why.

He went through the routine of the day, interviewing a couple of clients, preparing for cases that would go to court. He had heard nothing further from the Pincoles and wasn't sure whether they were still at logger-heads or in bed. The world beyond the horizon was still shuddering from the London bombings, the news out of Iraq was not improving and the price of oil was climbing steadily. There were major cracks in the wall of the world, but here in his suburban office the affairs of men and women were – well, suburban.

He went upstairs, heated up a ready-cooked meal in the microwave, took his time eating it, waited for her call. At 8 o'clock he called her at home, keeping his voice steady, as if facing a difficult client for the first time: 'You read my note?'

'Ye-es–' He noticed how she stretched the word as if it were written on elastic.

'Do you have any regrets?'

'No-o. But...'

'The worst word in the English language.

215

But. 'Even in his own ears he was starting to sound as if he was talking to a client.

'Joe, don't start sounding like a lawyer. I don't regret last night – do you?'

'No.' Emphatic.

'But–'

'Okay, yes. But. It was like old times, Lou, but one night doesn't make another honeymoon.'

'I couldn't have put it better myself,' she said, but her sarcasm was gentle. 'Give me time, Joe. Don't call me for another week...'

Then she hung up and he slowly replaced the receiver. He hadn't called her on his mobile; it was a necessary evil, but he hated it. The old handset, though he knew it was doomed, somehow still suggested permanence. And that was what he was looking for.

He got himself a light beer from the kitchen, went into the living room and sat for a while, taking sips of the beer and wondering how far he should step into the future.

Then he switched on the television and got a follow-up on the London bombings and the rising death toll. The world went round, everything kept in perspective.

Chapter Thirteen

1

Louise had lost her virginity at sixteen and it had been such a disastrous experience that she had been eighteen before she went all the way again. From then on she enjoyed sex, though she was not promiscuous; no more than in the new morality of the day (and night). She did not go in for one-night stands, which could be messy and even had their dangers; she looked for relationships. There had been three serious affairs before she met Joe, but she had discovered, too late, that none of the men wanted long-term commitment. Then Joe had come along, a practised lover; though he had never, even after they married, told her how and where he had practised. Similarly, she had never told him of her encounters; doors had been closed. It had taken her a little longer than him to fall genuinely in love, but once it had happened her surrender had been complete. The first few years of their marriage had made her happier than she had ever been. Then, as even now, she was not sure how it happened, things had begun to crumble.

They had gone to New Zealand on their honeymoon and there Joe had taught her to ski, a sport she had enjoyed till her pregnancy. She had not given up her job at Dampiers, though in those days there had been no Chapelli counter. She had worked on one of the standard cosmetic counters, assuring ageing matrons that glamour could still be found in a bottle. She had not taken maternity leave, because the miscarriage had occurred three months into the pregnancy. But there had been after-effects, including depression, and she had stayed home for almost six months. And in that time things had begun to worsen, though it would be another eighteen months before they talked of divorce.

She had no regrets about Wednesday night. They had made love twice, remembering the secrets of each other's bodies, then had fallen asleep. When she woke in the early morning he was gone and a little later the doubts had come back, like stains upon the sheets.

Out in the kitchen she had found his note, written in his usual strong hand. She had seen the sense of it; she, like him, had wanted no awkwardness. She didn't screw up the note, but took it back into the bedroom and put it in her bedside drawer. Like a keepsake.

She went to work, but business on the Chapelli counter was dead slow: two customers all day. Money, there was no doubt, was tightening. She closed down the counter at 5.30; though it was late-night shopping, the counter never remained open. Thursday night shoppers did not stop by for thousand-dollar purchases. She went home, made do with eggs and bacon for dinner, washed up and went in to look at the ABC 7 o'clock news. And, like Joe miles away, looked at scenes more immediately horrific than doubts about a relationship. But, of course, the doubts remained.

When he rang she had been cautious; to her, he had sounded the same. The voice has its inflections, but disembodied, over a phone or on a tape, it lacks the emphasis of facial expression. When she had hung up there was still a void between them.

Saturday came and she was glad she did not have to work; she worked one Saturday in three. She wanted today to herself; so, since there is nothing more isolating than vacuuming, she spent the morning cleaning the house. At lunchtime, hair under a shower-cap, no make-up, bra-less under an old baggy soccer sweater of Joe's, hips in even more baggy slacks, she took a plastic bag full of garbage down to the bins behind the flats.

There were no garages, just parking spaces for six cars on the concreted backyard. Benjamin Gelfman, from one of the ground-floor flats, was washing his car, an old Peugeot. There were still water restrictions and he was using water from a bucket instead of his usual hose.

He looked at her and said, straight-faced, 'You look nice. Going out?'

'In your eye, Ben. How's Grace?'

'Happy. She'll be babysitting this afternoon.' He and his wife had three sons and a daughter and six grandchildren.

'Here?'

'No, thank God. I want some peace and quiet. Grandkids are a treasure, but at a distance.'

He was in his early seventies, a lean, spry old man whose early life had left no visible marks. He had been born in Germany, fled from there with his parents to France ('I was two years old at the time, but decided to go with them'); then, when the Germans entered France, had gone on to England. From there he had emigrated to Australia in the 1950s, his parents in the meantime having died.

Louise had once asked him, 'Why Australia, Ben? Why not Israel?'

'I'm an atheist Jew – there aren't many of us, but some are. I didn't fancy life amongst the Orthodox. I read that sport was the Number One religion in Australia and I decided that was the place for me.'

'Did you ever play sport?'

'No, but I watched. I even developed the patience to watch cricket.' Then he had said, 'You're a Catholic?'

'A semi-lapsed one.' She had always felt awkward discussing religion. 'I've never met an atheist Catholic. We all seem to be lapsed, as if waiting to be asked back.'

Now she said as she pushed the garbage into a bin, 'Your shop's not open today?'

He had a small jeweller's shop over in Ashfield. 'My granddaughter is standing in. She's doing philosophy at university, says she's fascinated by time. So I'm giving her a morning amongst the watches and clocks.' He smiled, sloshed more water on the car. The car was at least ten to fifteen years old, but it looked new and she was sure it ran with the same precision as his watches and clocks. 'I don't understand the young. Do you?'

'Am I old?' He smiled again and shook his head and she went on, 'They don't have to be understood, Ben. Just tolerated. Who understood you when you were young?'

'I had different pressures,' he said chidingly and she blushed.

'Sorry.' She took off the shower cap, shook out her short hair.

'Oh, you've spoiled the effect!'

'In your eye again... My father once said Jews are the wisest people around–'

Ben Gelfman nodded. 'Jewish wisdom and Chinese wisdom, the two best in the world, the two oldest.'

'What about the Greeks and the Romans?'

'Too temperamental... What can I do for you?' He was now sponging the car.

'Nothing–' She flapped a hand, wondering why she had mentioned the subject. 'I just wonder why some things happen–'

'The bombings in London?'

She grasped that: 'Yes–'

He wrung out a chamois, took his time. 'History repeats itself, Louise. Innocent people die – it's in the Bible, Herod and the children... The concentration camps in Germany, Christians killed Muslims in Serbia...'

He gave the chamois an extra-tight squeeze. 'It's human nature–'

'What a cruel thing to say!'

'It's the truth, Louise. It's not Jewish wisdom, or Chinese – it's just the truth. Nobody does anything worse to men than other men. And sometimes women.'

'You sound as if you don't blame the terrorists in London–' She was sorry now that she had brought up the subject. Remote as most Australians, she did not understand terrorism.

'Of course I blame them!' He was angry now. 'But it's been happening ever since Cain slew Abel. When they dropped the atom bombs on Hiroshima and Nagasaki, had they thought about the thousands of women and children there?'

'There were German bombs on London–' Like most of her generation she had only a hazy knowledge of World War II. Her mother's father had fought in the Middle East and New Guinea, but he had died before she was born.

'Sure there were. But when the British bombed Dresden, killed thirty thousand civilians, did they think of them in advance? We've all committed sins, Louise, even the best of us. They say we Jews have the longest memories of us all. Maybe it's a punishment – there are fundamental Christians who still think that...' He squeezed the chamois tight again, stood for a moment, then looked at Louise. 'I'm sorry, Louise.'

'No–' She shook her head. 'It was my fault–'

'No.' He shook his head again, a mirror reflection. 'You are just the Lucky Australians.'

She hesitated, then nodded. She turned away to go back up to her flat and he said, 'You look beautiful–'

She looked back at him; he was smiling now. Then Grace Gelfman came round the corner, carrying a small basket of washing. 'What's he up to now? Telling more of his Jewish jokes?'

'No, he's flattering me. I'd watch him, Grace.'

Grace was a plain, plump woman in her sixties. She was not Jewish, but she had, or had acquired, dry Jewish humour. She began to hang out underwear, her own and her husband's. 'He's been doing that since I first met him. He says it's human nature.'

Louise looked at the old man, who smiled and spread his hands, a parody of a Jewish gesture.

'Have a nice day,' she said and went back up to her flat. She always enjoyed the Gelfmans, admired them. They, like her own mother and father had been, like Joe's parents were, were the knots that held the net of the nation together. Who had experience of human nature.

She stripped off, ready for a shower, wondering what she would do for the rest of the day and the evening, feeling suddenly lonely.

Then Marie, sounding distraught, phoned her.

Louise, standing naked, took the call on her mobile. 'What's the matter, Mar?'

'Are you on your own? Can I come over?'

'Of course. But what's the matter? You sound as if the roof has fallen in–'

'It has! I'll be there in half an hour. Just the two of us – okay?'

The phone went dead and Louise stood there. She dropped the phone on the bed, then suddenly she shivered. Not because she was naked and cold, but because Marie, her twin, had sounded anguished, almost terror-stricken. Not grief-stricken, as if something terrible had happened to Brigid or Rosie or Leif, but *terror*-stricken.

Chapter Fourteen

1

Marie didn't feel better on Saturday morning; she felt worse, much worse. *Sleep on anger:* she couldn't remember who had said or written that, but she would bet it hadn't been a woman. She got out of bed and went into the bathroom, shut the door and went through the monthly routine. She sluiced her face, paused and looked at herself in the mirror, at the stranger. She looked gaunt, older, but she knew she wasn't focussing properly. Then Leif knocked on the door.

'I come in?'

He always respected her privacy; he was almost old-fashioned about it. She opened the door, went to brush by him, but he put a soft hand on her shoulder.

'You feeling better?'

'No.' She was standing close to him, could feel the bed-heat of his body, wanted to break away. 'Take the girls to soccer and leave me to myself for a while–'

'You've never been as bad as this before–'

'No.' All at once she wanted to confront him, ask him for the truth about Dinah Camplin. But she brushed by him and then Rosie was in their bedroom, jumping up and down on the bed. 'I'll get breakfast. Come on, Rosie – *out!*'

'Mum, do I have to go to soccer? I wanna go skate-boarding – I saw it on TV – boys saying they were going arse-over-head–'

'Out!'

Somehow she got through breakfast without straining the atmosphere too much in front of the children. Leif looked at her curiously a couple of times, but said nothing. Then he kissed her on the cheek, the *old* Leif whom she loved, and took the girls off to soccer.

She didn't clear the breakfast table, just sat at it as if waiting for some sort of appointment – with whom? Then, bringing things to a head, she looked up Dinah Camplin's address in the phone book. She scribbled it down, pulled on a thick coat over her jeans and sweater, went out and got into the Corolla, sat for a moment, not wondering if she was doing the right thing, just steeling herself for it, then she started up the car and drove south towards – what? She wasn't sure, but the trip, the confrontation, had to be made.

It was a windy day, the clouds high in the sky as if pushed upwards. She drove over the Harbour Bridge, picked up the Eastern Distributor, drove steadily through it, feeling foreign. She came out into the open, still driving steadily, holding herself and the car in. Halfway to South Coogee she stopped and checked her street directory. Then she drove on, came to territory she had never visited before, no more than fifteen kilometres from her home or the suburb where she had grown up. Her first year out of university she had gone to Europe, come home through America; now she was in another foreign country. She found Dinah Camplin's street, drove up its hill but there were no parking spots and she went round the block and down onto the main road again.

She parked, sat for a few moments, then was aware of the cemetery across the road. Mourners stood around a grave that looked as if it had been reopened to take in the newly-dead; there was already a headstone above it, someone, a loved one, gone before. The bereaved stood in silence amongst the headstones; the wind blew from the south and a woman clutched at the large black hat she wore. Marie turned away, got out of the car and walked to the corner of Dinah's street, began to climb the hill. Her mind was blank of what she would do when Dinah opened her door. She clutched the earring in her coat pocket as if, producing it, she would not need to say anything.

She came to the address she had taken down. She was disturbed to find it was a small block of flats; she didn't want a scene with Dinah in front of a neighbour suddenly opening a front door. She would have to see she somehow got into the flat, faced Dinah behind a closed door.

Dinah lived on the ground floor. Marie pressed the doorbell and waited. What if the bitch wasn't at home? But almost immediately the door was opened. Dinah stood there in shorts and sweater, no make-up, rubber gloves on her hands.

'Yes? *Oh!*' There was no languid air to her now.

'Yes, oh!' said Marie and held up the earring. 'I come in?'

Dinah hesitated and looked for a moment as if she would slam the door shut. Marie, surprised at her own sudden determination, put her foot inside the doorway. 'Crush my foot and I'll scream the bloody place down!'

Dinah swung the door wide open and Marie walked in past her, stood while Dinah closed the door and, still silent, led the way into the small living room. Marie, without moving her head, looked around. It was better furnished than she had expected for a working girl. It was messy and untidy, as if a small party might have been held here last night. With Leif included?

The working girl, composure regained, was standing in front of her, taking off the rubber gloves. *As if expecting a bare-fist fight?* At school Marie had never been afraid of fights, from which Louise invariably had to rescue her.

'Thanks for bringing back my earring–'

'Did Leif take it off or did you and put it in his pocket?'

'Look, Marie–'

'Mrs Johnson.' Marie's voice was steady. 'Leif's wife. Has he been sleeping with you? Here?' She waved a hand around her.

Dinah took a sudden deep breath. 'Okay, let's get to the point. Yes, we've been to bed together, half a dozen times. If he doesn't get enough from you–'

The hand holding the earring moved of its own volition; there was no conscious thought behind the blow. It hit Dinah across the cheek and she staggered back. The next minute was a blur Marie would have trouble remembering. They clinched in a savage embrace; Dinah didn't retreat, she looked as if she wanted to fight. Fists flew, hands ripped like claws. They stumbled about the room, both of them cursing, gasping for breath, scratching and tearing at each other, Marie hampered by the coat she still wore. Then there was a frozen moment, they were separated, Dinah was back on her heels.

Marie swung her fist, not the one holding the earring. It was a boxer's punch. It hit Dinah square on the chin and she staggered back. Heir foot caught in a rug and she went over backwards in an awkward fall. Her head hit the corner of a bookcase with a gut-wrenching sound and she fell in a limp crumpled heap and lay still.

Marie, gasping for breath, looked down at her. She was trembling, her mind still a whirl, no thoughts in it. Then suddenly she realized the fight was over, that Dinah was unconscious, dead to the world. Tentatively, as if afraid Dinah would suddenly come to life and grab at her, she knelt down and touched the still face with the wide-open staring eyes. Almost automatically, she put a hand to Dinah's throat but even as she did she knew there would be no pulse. Dinah was dead.

She stood up on legs that seemed full of water, swayed, then caught her balance. She was not used to death; she had led a fortunate life. She had seen her mother dead, but that had been all. She looked down at Dinah and suddenly wanted to be sick; but managed to hold it back. Then, as if delayed, she felt the pain in the knuckles that had hit Dinah. She went to massage the hand with her other hand, then realized she was still holding the earring. Her hand opened as if the earring had cut her and she dropped it on the rug beside the body.

Then she jumped as a mobile somewhere rang; she saw it on a side table beside the couch. It rang and rang, not loudly but muted, and Marie stood stockstill waiting for it to stop. Then it did and the room was silent again.

Her mind still not functioning, not knowing why she did it, she bent and picked up the earring, put it in her coat pocket; as if it were some sort of visiting card, her own. She turned to go, suddenly wanting to be out of the flat and at home, when she saw the book on top of the small bookcase. It was a copy of *Barney's Bank Job*, her name there on the jacket like a bright neon sign.

She grabbed it, looked inside: there was no inscription. She took it with her, as if it were incriminating evidence, as she let herself out of the flat, pulling the front door quietly behind her. Her fingerprints on the doorbell and the door handle were the only evidence she left.

Unobserved, she went out of the flats and down the steep hill, forcing herself to walk unhurriedly so as not to attract attention. She passed a couple of people, but they were engrossed in themselves and did not look at her. The wind came through a gap between two houses and tore at her; her eyes bleared with tears. Then she had come to her car.

She got in, closed the door and all at once began to shake. She closed her eyes, afraid of fainting, and slowly the shaking subsided. She opened her eyes, looked across the road to the cemetery. The mourners were moving away from the grave, taking away grief and memory. The wind seemed suddenly to increase, like the Fates shouting, and the woman in the large black hat lost it; it blew away amongst the headstones, like a great black bird, and a small boy went after it, jumping graves, dodging amongst the stone angels as if in a game. Marie started up the car and drove away from death and its aftermath.

A kilometre further on, still in foreign territory, she stopped the car, but kept the engine running. She took her mobile from the glovebox, hesitated, then punched in Louise's number.

2

'Why the hell did you go to see her?'

'Don't bark at me, Lou – *please!* I dunno why I went. I've got my period, I felt lousy and angry–'

'Did anyone see you go in? A neighbour or someone?'

'No, I don't think so–'

'Why didn't you have it out with Leif first? Show him the earring and hear what he had to say?'

'I dunno.' She shook her head, still adrift on emotion. 'Maybe I was scared he would tell me he loved her, not me–'

Leif wouldn't have done that; Louise knew that for a fact. 'Bullshit. He loves you. He was just dipping his wick, the way men do–' It was vulgar, the way they had been when they were twenty, being *with it*. 'I think you should have had it out with him–'

They were in Louise's kitchen, sitting round the corner of the table from each other, each with a cup of coffee in front of her, the antidote that never did anything despite the claims of Starbucks and Gloria Jean's. The wind, following Marie, brushed angrily against the windows; then, as if for emphasis, hurled rain against the glass. All we need now, thought Louise irrelevantly, is thunder and lightning.

'I couldn't, Lou. What if we'd had a terrible row in front of the girls? They're the ones I'm thinking of–' It had only just occurred to her; but it was true. 'They'd of heard us–'

Louise nodded, suddenly wanting Brigid and Rosie to be protected, as if they were her own. 'No, we've got to keep it from them... You say you hit her?'

'Yes – on the chin. We were like those girls in those awful wrestling shows–' She shook her head again. 'She fell backwards, she must've caught her heel on the rug – the next thing–' She closed her eyes, hearing that terrible *clump*.

'If the police find out about you – I mean, you going to see her – they'll charge you with – I think it's called involuntary manslaughter. I've heard Joe mention it–'

'Do you think I should go to the police?'

Louise took her time: 'Morally, I'd say yes. Sensibly, I'd say no.'

Then Marie suddenly broke down, began to weep in deep racking sobs. Louise moved round to her, put her arms round her, held her close. They were twins again, not merely sisters. The wind suddenly dropped, the rain gone; everything around them was silent.

At last Marie drew back, wiped her eyes. 'What am I going to do?'

Louise, over the initial shock, was taking charge; as she had in their childhood and teens: 'Give me the earring–'

'Why? It's in the pocket of my coat–'

'Because I don't want you doing something bloody stupid with it – like suddenly deciding to show it to Leif–'

'He'll have to know eventually–'

'We'll wait till then – sometimes eventually never comes. Give it to me.' Marie reached for her coat, took out the earring and handed it over. Louise looked at it: 'What is it?'

'It's a zodiac sign – Virgo–'

'Virgo? God, what a joke!' She turned the earring over in her hand. 'Forget you ever saw this–'

'That's easier said than done–' Marie now was quieter, calmer.

'I know how it's going to be. But as you said – Brigid and Rosie are the important ones in this–'

Marie shook her head mournfully. 'Oh, God, everything was going to be great!'

'Get through the weekend somehow without letting Leif – or the girls – know how you feel. Work your period for sympathy–'

For a moment Marie was angry again: 'How can you be so bloody calm? As if nothing's happened?'

'I'm not calm and I know something's happened. But I'm trying to hold us together. You and me and the girls and Leif, too.'

'I don't care a bugger about him–'

'Yes, you do. Or you wouldn't have gone out this morning to have it out with Whatshername–'

Marie suddenly smiled; it was wan, almost a grimace, but it was a smile. 'You should've been a marriage counsellor–'

'If I had been, I might've saved mine. You want more coffee?'

Chapter Fifteen

1

Leif had spent an unhappy weekend. There had been one or two occasions in the past when Marie had been miserable and bad-tempered from her period; but that mood had not lasted as deeply and as long as this one. He had wondered if all the excitement of the past month, the interviews, the thought of all the success on the horizon, had upset her system.

'Do you think that could be it?' he asked her on the Saturday night.

'It could be. Probably.'

She had never been as distant, as remote from him as this. He was tender with her and though she did not snap at him or push him away, she was nothing like *his* Marie. She was patient with the girls, but only just.

Sunday afternoon he suggested they go for a drive up to the northern beaches – 'have a nice afternoon tea somewhere, give the girls a treat' – but she had said no, she just wanted to rest. In the end they had stayed home and he had mowed the lawn and done some gardening, not one of his usual pleasurable activities. But it got him out of the house, away from her, and he was ashamed that he thought that way.

Monday morning he got dressed for the office. 'When will that other suit be back from the cleaners?'

'I'll pick it up this afternoon, when I pick up the girls.'

'You feeling a bit better this morning?'

'A little,' she said and offered her cheek for his kiss. 'A day or two and I'll be okay.'

'I hope so,' he said. 'I love you, Mar–'

'I know. I love you, too.'

Brigid stood in the doorway of her bedroom looking at them. 'I like it when you're in love.'

'What do you know about love?' said Leif, smiling.

'Miss Gibson, at school, tells us about it–'

Leif looked at Marie. 'How progressive can a school be?'

She smiled and he kissed her again and left.

He had been in his office only ten minutes when Steve Perkins sent for him. Now they were no longer a ministry, where they had

had their own building, the Office of Intra-Urban Development had only a floor in one of the grand old sandstone buildings that had housed government ministries and departments over the last hundred and fifty years. Woodwork gleamed from decades of polishing, the ceilings were high enough to breed their own shadows; the atmosphere was quiet, as if the building itself was a reminder that ministries and ministers come and go, most of the ministers no longer remembered. Leif wondered if Steve Perkins ever absorbed any of the atmosphere.

'Oh, Leif–' Perkins looked up as Leif knocked and entered his office. It was a smaller office than the one he had occupied in the ministry, but not small enough to demean him. The dignity of its years was like a benediction. 'The Premier has just given us a new job–'

Leif sat down. 'Doing what?'

'He wants a small unit put together that will handle all the terrorist business. What happened in London last week has put the shits up everyone. Eventually, if we and Canberra get off our arses, there'll be a central outfit, the states and Canberra. Like that American thing, Homeland Security–'

'I've been reading about it. Twenty-two

agencies and 180,000 personnel. Don't they get in each other's way?'

'Well, forget that. The Premier's got it into his head that he'll be carrying the flag–'

'With a sniffer dog on a lead?'

'Don't put this down, Leif–'

'I'm not, Steve. But why wasn't all this started a coupla years ago, a year or so ago after the Madrid bombing?'

'Leif, you never frighten the chickens or the voters. But now it's serious. I want you to get together a group, half a dozen or so at the most, and we'll have a meeting tomorrow, nut out a preliminary programme.'

'What do you or I or any of us know about terrorism?'

'Bugger-all, Leif. Now's when we start learning. And praying–' He looked at Leif hopefully.

'I'll try and remember a few prayers–'

He went back to his office, was there only five minutes, when a girl from the computer pool appeared in his doorway: 'Mr Johnson, these two gentlemen would like to see you–'

They were both about Leif's age, sober-suited, sober-faced. 'Detective-Constable Mendez and Detective-Constable Stephen.' The one who had spoken produced a police badge. 'May we come in?'

'Of course. Thank you–' But he couldn't remember the girl's name, she was new. Then he remembered she had replaced Dinah on Friday afternoon, come from another department. 'Come in. What's the problem? Not terrorism? I've just had a session with my boss – are we going to be working with you?'

'I don't think so, Mr Johnson. Or maybe you will be–' They sat down, not awkwardly but at ease, part of their daily routine. Mendez was dark and handsome and had a soft approach: 'You knew a Miss Dinah Camplin?'

'Yes, she was in our computer pool, one of the girls there. But she's left. Is she in trouble of some sort?' He couldn't imagine what sort of trouble she could get herself into. He had never met, in all the girls he had known, one as self-contained as she was.

'No–' D.C Stephen was big, as big as Leif himself; he was not fat, but looked as if he was outgrowing his suit. 'It's bad news, I'm afraid. Miss Camplin is dead, her body was discovered Saturday afternoon in her flat in South Coogee.'

'Jesus!' Leif blinked, sat very still in his chair. 'How? I mean, how did she die?'

Stephen didn't answer that, but Mendez said, 'How well did you know her?'

Leif was cautious, but tried not to sound it: 'I didn't know her well, she was just one of the girls in the pool. When she left I wrote her a reference–'

'We thought you might've known her,' said Mendez. 'She had a photo of you in a drawer beside her bed.'

'Of me?' He was genuinely surprised; he had always been careful not to leave traces of himself in the bedrooms he had visited. 'Like I said, I hardly knew her–'

'It was a newspaper photograph,' said, Stephen. 'She'd evidently cut it out and kept it. Did she have a crush on you?'

Leif knew all at once that he had to tread carefully. He was certain they had kept their affair secret. She had not been close to any of the girls in the pool; she had never been one for office gossip, never mentioning anything she had heard. But you never knew... 'I told you, I hardly knew her. Once, back when we were a ministry, she worked with me for one night at a reception. But it was "Mr Johnson", "Miss Camplin", nothing more than that.'

'Why did she leave here Friday? The girls in your computer pool said she left suddenly.'

'You've been talking to them? You don't think you should've come to me first?' He was afraid, but managed to make it sound angry.

'You weren't here, Mr Johnson,' said Stephen. 'They said you were with the minister. We were just saving time–'

'Why did she leave suddenly?' asked Mendez again.

'She'd been offered another job – I guess it was better pay. And we're in a – a state of flux here. Getting used to the idea we're no longer a ministry.'

'We know how you feel, Mr Johnson. It's like that with us, changes all the time... The reference you gave her was in the bedside drawer with your photo. It was a good one.'

'You do that with references, don't you? Make them sound good.'

'I wouldn't know,' said Stephen. 'Have you, Carl?'

'Never,' said Mendez.

Leif kept his voice steady. 'How did she – did she die?'

'It looks as if she fought with someone,' said Mendez. 'It could have been an intruder, though there was no sign of a break-in. It looks as if she was knocked backwards, there was a bruise on her chin, she fell over and hit her head. Nothing was stolen from her flat–'

'You'd never been to her flat?' said Stephen.

'I told you–' Then Leif tightened the rein on himself. 'I have no idea where she lived.'

'South Coogee,' said Mendez.

'I don't think I've been to South Coogee in my life. Look, I tell you – I hardly knew her. She was attractive, I think a lot of guys might've looked at her, but as far as I know, she never stirred up anything in the office. It's a shock, what happened to her–'

Mendez and Stephen suddenly stood up, as if there was a silent signal between them. 'I don't think we'll have to bother you again, Mr Johnson. But just for the record – where were you Saturday morning?'

Leif frowned; his mind kept slipping out of gear. 'Saturday morning? I was with my two girls, they play soccer–'

'Detective Mendez plays soccer, he's a goalkeeper,' said Stephen. 'Only he calls it football, as if it's the only game.'

Leif stood up, didn't move out from behind his desk; he couldn't trust his legs. 'I'll have someone see you out–'

'Don't bother,' said Mendez. 'We'll see ourselves out. We're used to it.' And they were gone.

Leif slumped back into his chair, sat there for several minutes without moving. Then he looked up as Jill Bessemer came into his

245

office. 'The girls tell me a coupla cops came to see you. They already in this anti-terrorist set-up that we haven't yet started?'

'No,' he said, his voice dry in his throat. 'Dinah Camplin is dead.'

Jill blinked, sat down. 'The girls didn't tell me that. How? Why come here, the police?'

Leif told her what the police had told him, but left out the bit about his photograph and the reference letter in Dinah's bedside drawer. 'They don't appear to have any leads. They just asked me what I knew of her background. How much did you or any of the girls know about her?'

'Virtually nothing. She was a bit stand-offish, I mean as far as we women went. But not as far as the men. Did they ask to see any of the men?'

'No. Did you–' He put the question, though he knew the answer. 'Did you ever see her flirting with any of the guys?'

'Flirting? That's a word I haven't heard since my grandmother died... No. She swung her hips and she looked – is available the word I want? – but I never saw her holding hands with any of the guys. I didn't like her, but it's upsetting to know she's dead. Violently?'

'So the police said. Let the girls in the pool

know what the police told me. They'll be upset, but it's better they hear it from you than read it in the papers.'

Jill stood up. 'You look washed out–'

He shook his head. 'It's not Dinah, though that's a shock. Marie hasn't been well – I've been playing mother and father to our girls–'

'Marie must be run off her feet, promoting her book. How's it going?'

'Just keeps getting bigger and bigger–'

'The new Harry Potter is published this week. I read that the American publishers have printed eight or nine million copies.'

He managed a smile. 'Marie is not in that class. If she were I wouldn't be sitting here–'

Jill suddenly looked wistful, an expression not common to her. 'I wonder what it's like to be as successful as that Rowling woman? Or the *Da Vinci Code* man?'

'We'll never know, Jill.'

The wistful expression died, as if it knew it was a stranger to her face. 'No... I'll tell the girls about Dinah.'

Leif spent the rest of the day in a cocoon; of doubt and trepidation. What if Dinah had told a friend or a sister (she had a sister somewhere) of their affair? His photograph, even if just a newspaper photo, in her bedside table worried him. He left his office early and drove home carefully, as if every road might have a disaster at its end. He put the car away, closed the garage door and stood looking at the fading day. The tibouchina looked anonymous, its colour gone. It was midwinter, but the day was not gloomy. There was no wind and the sky was cloudless; it was a mockery of his feelings. Then the girls came round the side of the house, rushed at him as they always did, and once again, as he so often did, he felt the comfort of home. Conscience, and fear, bit at him like snapping locks.

He went into the house, carrying Rosie on his back, Brigid hanging on to his jacket, and Marie turned from the kitchen bench, where she was slicing vegetables, and raised an eyebrow.

'You're early–'

He nodded, slid Rosie off his back and pushed her and Brigid towards the kitchen door. 'Go and look at the cartoons. I'll be in in a minute–'

The girls left the kitchen and he looked at Marie. 'You feeling a little better?'

She nodded, gave him her cheek for his kiss. 'A little. Why so early?'

He draped his jacket over a chairback, carefully, as if the chair had to be dressed impeccably. Then he faced her and said, 'Remember Dinah, the girl who babysat for us? She worked for our office?'

Marie had been slicing a carrot; the knife suddenly stopped. 'What about her?'

'She's dead. The police came to see me today – they don't think it was an accident, they think she had a fight with someone, fell over and cracked her head–'

Marie frowned, the knife still steady in her hand. 'Why did they come to see you?'

He was lying, but in a good cause, he told himself. 'They were checking if she had any sort of relationship with anyone in the office.'

'Had she?'

'As far as we know, no.'

Marie began slicing the carrot again. 'Don't let's talk about it in front of the girls. Don't mention her.'

'No.' He stroked the back of her neck. 'I'm glad you're feeling better.'

'It's not over yet,' she said and he wondered why she sounded a little abstracted.

Chapter Sixteen

1

Out beyond the office windows the day was bright with sun, not in the least cold-looking; where was winter? Out on the wide street beyond the ornamental gates an oil tanker went past, closely trailed by three cars, like metal ferrets waiting to attack. On the far footpath a squad of pupils from a nearby school of performing arts skipped along, future stars, future flops, promises, promises...

In the office Joe was interviewing the girl who had assaulted her boyfriend. Her mother was with her.

'Let's see what you did to–' He looked at the papers on his desk. 'To Jamie... Fractured skull, fractured cheekbone, two broken ribs, bruises, lacerations... How? How did you do all that damage?'

'With my hockey stick. I was on my way home from hockey practice when I met him.'

She was not what Joe had expected. She was a good-looking girl, in the uniform of one of the best-known private girls' schools. She was composed and, as far as Joe could tell, not in the least remorseful about what she had done.

'He's a bastard, a cad, as they used to say–' The mother had been plain but had been dragged over the line by money, beauty parlours and an expensive costumier. She had a good figure, sculpted by a personal trainer, wore a beige two-piece suit and a brown silk shirt. She carried a crocodile-skin handbag and wore matching shoes. She was no animal lover nor, it seemed, a lover of boys who left her daughter in the lurch. As they used to say. 'He treated Sophie like a slut–'

'Mum, let me tell it–' The girl had a soft pleasant voice, the vowels rounded. She should be reciting poetry, Joe thought, not abuse.

'Go ahead,' said Joe. 'Have you had any other boyfriends?'

'What sort of question is that?' demanded the mother.

'If we go to court, that's the sort of question Jamie's lawyers are going to ask. Did you, Sophie?'

'Yes.' She was not at all hesitant. 'But I never went all the way with any of them. Jamie was the first, the only one. When I told him I was pregnant, he said, was I sure, couldn't it have been someone else?'

'Are you on the Pill?' asked Joe, with a wary eye on the mother.

'I was, but I'd forgotten that week. When he asked couldn't it have been someone else, that was when I did my block and hit him. Then I kept hitting him–'

'All the girls at her school are on her side,' said the mother.

Joe had a mental picture of rows and rows of girls in their school uniforms cheering on the sidelines as at a hockey match.

'I don't think that will carry much weight with a judge or a magistrate. How are Jamie's parents treating it?'

'His mother wants Sophie sent to gaol. But his father, we think, wants to back off. He's the CEO of–' She named one of the city's best-known firms. 'I think its a macho thing. He doesn't want his son named as a namby-pamby who let a girl beat him up.'

Joe sighed inwardly. 'Mrs Purdell, the fact of the matter is that she *did* beat him up.' He gestured at the papers on his desk. 'Those injuries are not just a black eye and one or two bruises. She could've killed him.'

He looked at the girl, who said, 'That was the way I felt at the time.'

'How have the police treated you when questioning you?'

Sophie took her time; Joe was still marvelling at her composure. 'Sympathetically, I think. I was interviewed by two women police.'

'They understood,' said Mrs Purdell, certain of the solidarity of women.

Joe couldn't see two policewomen beating Jamie with their truncheons, but he made no comment. 'I think our best hope is that Jamie's father prevails and they ask for the case not to go ahead. Does your husband know Jamie's father?' Joe knew that at the top level in Sydney business everyone at least waved to each other.

'They sit together on a couple of boards.'

Joe looked at Sophie. 'Are you going to have the baby?'

'Yes.' Still composed. 'Mum and I have talked it over – I don't want an abortion.'

'What about Jamie?'

'Stuff him,' said Sophie in her best private school accent and her mother nodded.

Joe sat forward. It had suddenly occurred to him, like a key pressed on a register, that seventy per cent of his clients were women. How did I get into this? he wondered, I'm not a ladies' man. 'Look, Sophie, I'm on your side. Not just because I'm your lawyer, but because I understand why you lost your temper–'

'Do you have children?' asked Mrs Purdell.

'No.' He offered no more than that. 'Sophie, we'll brief a top barrister–' He looked at her mother, where the money was apparent: 'Okay with you?'

'The very top. Don't worry about what it'll cost.'

'Right, that's what we'll do. In the meantime we can only hope that Jamie's dad is the one who'll prevail.' He was not a macho fan, but in law you fell back on any support.

'It's his mother who's got all the say,' said Sophie's mother.

Joe couldn't imagine one of the city's top businessmen coming home to be told to shut up and be quiet. 'Is Jamie a namby-pamby type?'

'No-o,' said Sophie, wavering for a moment. 'He was very macho – he was always being sent off the field playing rugby. That was what I liked about him – at first.'

Joe was beginning to think Sophie had a little blood-lust in her. Head-stomping in rugby, assault with a hockey stick… 'Did he try to attack you when you first went for him?'

'He didn't stand a chance,' said Sophie, Boadicea in a school uniform. 'The first hit was his skull–'

Joe mentally shuddered; then, almost sighing, said, 'Sophie, don't talk like that if we get into court. You play the bewildered little girl spurned by this lout who accused you of being loose with your favours.' *What am I saying?*

'Exactly what I told her,' said Mrs Purdell. 'In different words.'

'When's the baby due?'

'March,' said Sophie, calm as if it were just another birthday present. 'I sit for my HSC in November and I was hoping to start uni next year.'

'Doing what?'

Sophie smiled, the first time since coming into Joe's office. 'I hope to be a doctor.' Then she was very sober: 'Will I go to gaol?'

'I don't know. If we get a misogynistic judge, you may. On the other hand, you may get a suspended sentence, maybe eighteen months or two years.'

'If I go to court, all the girls in my class have said they'll be there.'

Just what we need, said Joe to himself. But aloud he said, 'I'll look forward to it.'

2

When Sophie and her mother had gone, Joe didn't ring for Edith but sat on with his own thoughts, which had nothing to do with the Purdell case. He had waited for a call from Louise, but there had been none. *Don't call me for another week*, she had said. He was patient, always had been, but love eats at patience like a voracious beast. He knew he could not last a whole week without hearing from her. Today was only Monday; he would give her till Wednesday at the latest. Then, if he hadn't heard from her, he would call. He would have to...

It was ten minutes before Edith knocked on his door and came in. He always found it reassuring to look on her: she was common-sense in a blue twinset and sensible shoes. 'How'd it go?'

'What?' He was still thinking of Louise; then he recovered: 'Our little girl should go into politics. With her hockey stick she'd clean up some of those squabbling MPs... I don't know, Edie. The trouble is she's showing no sign of being sorry for what she did–'

'I'm with her. But don't quote me.'

'–she's talking of having the whole of her HSC class in court with her, if we get that far. Can you imagine how that will go down with some of our old codger judges?'

'It might shake 'em up a bit. Some of them could do with it.'

'I think you're the opposite of a misogynist. Is there a word for it?'

'Feminist will do, though I dunno I'm one of those, either... Mr and Mrs Pincole are outside, want to know if you can give them ten minutes?'

'Daggers still drawn? I'm not in the mood for any more of that.'

'No, they're lovebirds. It's disgusting, they're crawling all over each other. Shanyne is goggle-eyed, looks as if she's watching a porno movie.'

'You two seem to have more fun out there in the outer office than I do in here. Okay, send 'em in, but stand by in case I call for help.'

The Pincoles came in holding hands. Mrs Pincole looked as if she had put on a kilo or two; Harold Pincole looked as if he had lost weight. The beam of their smiles was almost blinding, a reflection of the sunlight outside.

'We've come to thank you, Mr Fernandez,' said Mrs Pincole; or rather, she trilled. This is like one of those awful British comedies on the ABC in the middle of the night, thought Joe. 'You brought us together again–' Even the dialogue sounded the same.

'You saved our marriage,' said Harold and made it sound as if the *Titanic* had missed the iceberg.

Joe tried to look modest. 'That's part of our job. Bind as well as separate.' Where had he heard that? He was starting to pontificate, like Felix Aylmer back in 1934 and black-and-white. 'What's the future?'

'I've taken a job with Sydney Ferries, their chief engineer.'

'He'll be home every night,' said Mrs Pincole, breathless. 'And all weekend!' The exclamation mark was so pronounced it was as if she had painted it on the air. Then she lifted up a paper satchel and put it on Joe's desk. 'A bottle of Bollinger, as our thanks. I paid for it out of housekeeping,' she told her husband and gave him a smile that threatened to devour him. 'We're so grateful, Mr Fernandez!'

Joe took the bottle from the satchel, then reached across his desk and shook hands with both of them; their hands felt clammy, as if they had been molesting each other before they came in, to Shanyne's fascination. 'I'll drink your health and your happiness.'

'And we'll drink yours,' said Harold and they went out of the office, headed, Joe knew, for bed.

Edith appeared at his door again. 'They're back together?'

'He's come ashore. He's got a job with Sydney Ferries.'

'I don't think I'll travel by ferry for a while.' She looked at the bottle on his desk. 'Champagne – they gave you that? Do I send 'em a bill?'

'Of course. I'm a lawyer, not a social worker.'

'You're more versatile than you think.'

She went out and Joe lolled back in his chair. He did not feel versatile; he was feeling lonely. There had been loneliness during the separation from Louise; then with the divorce there had been a feeling of release. He had not gone on a sexual carnival; there had been two other women, but they had not been looking for anything permanent. Then those affairs had petered out, amicably, and since then there had been a couple of one-night stands, but they had been no more satisfactory than paying for a night with a hooker. He had been celibate for three months, despite the temptation of Sharon on the floor below, and he had begun to feel like St Francis of Assisi, content to feed the birds, the feathered sort.

Then last Wednesday night had been a reminder how much he had been missing Louise. It was not just the sex, but the comfort of closeness, the saying nothing because nothing needed to be said. It was the nature of love.

Edith and Shanyne had left for the day and he was tidying up his desk when his phone rang. It was Louise: 'Joe, can I come and see you?'

'Here?'

'Yes–'

There was something in her voice that was distant: 'What's the matter, Lou?'

'I'll tell you when I see you.'

He put down the phone, puzzled and worried. Out beyond the windows the sky had darkened, like someone closing a huge lid.

Chapter Seventeen

1

Louise had had a worrying, miserable week-end. When she and Marie had come out of the flats Saturday morning, Ben Gelfman had been picking dead blooms from the two rows of azaleas that he cultivated to line either side of the front path.

'Ben, you've met my sister–'

'Indeed I have.' He had an Old World courtesy, a little worn round the edges by local influence. 'I read your book to one of my grandchildren. You have a fine criminal mind.'

Louise felt Marie stiffen beside her; but Marie recovered, managed a smile. 'It's a children's book, Mr Gelfman. They don't take the world as seriously as we do–'

'I know that. But the planning of the crime... Why is it that so many of the best crime writers are women? I've often wondered what it would be like to have lived with Agatha Christie. I'd have had a food taster in the house, for fear she was experimenting with poisons.'

'Women writers are not as bad as that,' said Louise, sensing Marie did not want to get into any discussion about crime, poisoning or otherwise. 'They're never as brutal as men writers.'

Gelfman picked a brown bloom from a bush. 'That's the subtlety of you women.' Then he gave Marie his lovely smile: 'Good luck with your book. Get rich – it's better.'

Louise took Marie out to the Corolla. 'You're going to have to be careful from now on. People may say the wrong thing – unintentionally.'

'I dunno I'm going to be able to weather it–'

'You *have* to–' Louise put her into the car, leaned in the open window. 'Keep your mouth shut – especially towards Leif. Don't, for God's sake, even hint at what happened.'

'What if he brings it up? He'll learn about it, read something – she worked for him–'

'Play dumb. Mar–' She put her hand on Marie's arm. 'This isn't just between you and him. Keep repeating that to yourself – it's for Brigid and Rosie. They're the ones to be protected – not you or Leif and your feelings about him and his slut–'

'But I killed her!'

'No, you didn't. Not if what you told me is true – she fell and hit her head–'

'But I *wanted* to hurt her! I hit her – as hard as I could–'

'Go home. Keep your mouth shut and I'll be in touch.'

She watched Marie drive away, wondering if she herself should not have taken her home. Then she turned and went into the front garden, where Ben Gelfman was still plucking dead blooms from the azaleas.

He looked at the flowers, then at her and smiled again. 'The thing I like about flowers is that they renew their beauty every year. A pity we humans can't do the same.'

She was in no mood for humour, but she said, 'Are you getting at me, Ben?'

'Never. I'd always rather look at women than flowers.'

'He's at it again,' said Grace from their front bedroom window and Louise went into the flats with a laugh that was almost like an aspirin of relief.

She got through the rest of the day with difficulty. Not for the first time, she felt the weight of living alone. Though she tried to distract herself with chores, washing her underwear, doing some ironing, her mind kept escaping from the flat. She kept thinking of Marie and the skirting of Leif, trying not to tell him what had happened. After a supper that she hadn't tasted, she watched television: the death toll from the London bombings was rising. But other people's misery, at a distance, doesn't outweigh one's own. All at once she felt lonely, was tempted to call Joe; but Marie's secret was still too close, she wasn't ready to open it up, even to someone as sympathetic as Joe would be. She went to bed and slept fitfully, even though exhausted. She woke once and somewhere out in the darkness a girl screamed, then laughed as if in hysterics. She went back to sleep, wondering what sound Marie had made when she realized that Whateverher-namewas was dead.

Sunday morning she went to Mass, sat in a back pew and prayed. Prayer, once taught, remains embedded; it may wilt, crumble in the fingers of unbelief, but it is always there. She didn't go to Communion, aware of sins she did not regret. The sermon was as bland and hoary as those she had heard as a child; time had stood still in certain elements of the Church. But the hour was a retreat and she went back to her flat, if not refreshed, at least sustained. Because she knew now that

Marie was going to be leaning on her. They were together again in another womb.

Late in the morning she rang Marie's mobile, not wanting Leif to pick up her call. But it was answered by Brigid: 'Auntie Lou! Oh, it's nice to talk to you!'

'How are you, pet?'

'Lousy–' Brigid had announced that she was going to be an actress, play the lead in *Neighbours* or, better still, *Desperate Housewives*. 'Mum's not well, Dad's in a bad mood, Rosie thinks her teeth are falling out and I think I'm getting pneumonia.'

'God, what a miserable lot you are! Why do you think you're getting pneumonia?'

'I've got this tickle in my throat – I can hardly breathe – oh, here's Mum! Come and see me when I'm in hospital–'

'Sure, Camille–'

'Who?'

'Forget it. Put Mum on...' Marie came on the air and Louise said, 'How are things? Is Leif there?'

'He's out in the garden reading the week-end newspapers... I'm okay.'

'You sound as if you're at the bottom of a well–'

'How do you expect me to sound?' There was silence for a moment, then she said

265

more softly, 'Sorry.'

'I've just been talking to the drama queen. But she and Rosie are the reasons – well, we talked about that yesterday. Have you still got your period?'

'Yes–'

'Well, make the most of it till you're more settled. Nature must have given them to us for some reason. You know what I mean–'

'I'll never be able to let him again–'

'Balls, Marie. It'll happen and you'll have to make the best of it. Close your eyes and think of Mother England–'

'What?'

'I read that somewhere, it was the advice English mothers used to give to their daughters on their wedding night, back in Victorian times–' To her surprise there was a giggle at the other end of the airwaves. 'There – you can at least still manage a laugh.'

'I'll have to manage much more than that – I've never done it with my eyes closed–'

What are we saying? It was like their confidences of years ago, when they had first started experiencing boys. 'Eyes open or closed, think of Brigid and Rosie – okay? Eyes open and mouth shut.'

'I love you, sis–'

'Same here. Give my love to Leif,' she said automatically.

'You're kidding—' But then Marie clicked off her phone.

Louise hung up her phone, looked at it, wondered if she should call Joe. Then decided against it; his was the sort of calm outlook that was needed. But not yet.

Monday was a good day at the Chapelli counter, as if those with money to spare had decided the end of the world was nigh and they had better spend the moolah while they had it. The organist on the Wurlitzer apparently caught what was in the air; or anyway, the air over the Chapelli counter. He played old Irving Berlin numbers; the chandeliers rocked to 'Alexander's Ragtime Band'. Louise sold two seven-thousand-dollar watches and enough top-of-the-range perfume to have sent a harem into a swoon. It was ridiculous, but money, on its own, has no sense. One buyer was from the Philippines, the other from Dubai. The local money, spoiled now by so many bargain sales, waited for the watches, the perfume and the earrings to have 50 per cent off. But Chapelli never indulged the penny-pinching public. Its last sale had been in Florence in 1793, the year the Arno flooded and damaged some goods.

At her lunchbreak Louise rang Marie from the staffroom. 'How are you holding up?'

'Just,' said Marie and sounded on the verge of tears. In the past she had always seemed and sounded strong, but now she was crumbling.

'I've been thinking–' She was keeping her voice low as other women came into the big room. 'We need some legal advice–'

'No! Lou, please – who are you thinking of? Joe? I don't want him to know–'

'Mar, this isn't something that's going to go away, like some domestic argument. I'm trying to help you, for God's sake–'

'I know, Lou. I know, and I'm grateful. But I dunno what to do–'

'Just don't let Leif know. It's going to be a long road, Mar – that's why I think we may need some help, some advice... I've got to go, it's getting crowded here–'

She hung up and Mira was suddenly beside her, happy as ever, not a care in menswear. 'Lou, you look – what's the word? Peaked? How's business?'

'Good, today. Terrible, last week. How're things in menswear?' Another country.

'Fair. I'm enjoying it, the young guys on the floor are so friendly. So far I haven't got to take any inside-leg measurements.'

'Keep trying. It's the direct route to a man's heart.'

She sold one more bottle of perfume the rest of the day, to a girl who looked as if she would spray most of it on herself while on her back. The Chapelli counter, Louise had decided long ago, catered for sin.

Then at 6 o'clock, back in the staffroom, she called Joe.

2

Joe had been waiting for her, watching from his front window, and he was down at the front door of the big house when she came up the steps.

'By taxi?' he said. 'Such extravagance.'

'All the way from Dampiers—'

He kissed her cheek and led her across the wide front hall as Sharon came out of the doctor's surgery. Louise looked at Joe out of the corner of her eye to see if he was embarrassed; but he wasn't.

'You two remember each other—'

'Of course,' said Sharon, sounding as if she and Louise had met in a wrestling match. 'It's nice to see you together again.'

'Purely professional,' said Louise. 'He's still my legal adviser.'

'And who better?' said Sharon and went on out into the cold evening.

As they climbed the wide stairs, some of which creaked with age, Louise said, 'Don't you find it awkward, her working so close to you?'

'Lou, that barbecue was the first time I'd asked her anywhere. She read more into it – and so did you.' They had reached the door of his flat. 'Do you want to go out to dinner, we'll talk there?'

'No, here... Can I have a drink?'

He had not seen her as tightly wound as this since the days just before their divorce became final. 'I have some champagne–'

'No, this isn't a champagne occasion. Something stronger – vodka-and-tonic?'

He frowned, but made no comment other than, 'Sure. More vodka than tonic?'

He went out to the kitchen and she sat down in the big living room and looked around her. The furnishings were not to her taste, but they were comforting. Well, some of them were. On the wall opposite her was a long pike, hung slantwise, point down. Below it was an elaborate saddle on a clothes-horse. On the polished teak coffee table, bought, she guessed, secondhand, was a copy of *House & Garden*, its cover featuring an all-white room. All white: walls, carpet, couch, chairs and a glass coffee table with corners as menacing as a shark's teeth. Cold as an operating theatre, one for dissection, not sympathy. She took another look around Joe's room and decided she was in the right place.

Joe came back with a vodka-and-tonic and a light beer for himself. He seated himself opposite, taking his time as if she were a new client, and said gently, 'Okay, what's your problem?'

'Not mine–' She sipped her drink, took the plunge: 'It's Marie–'

Then she told him everything that Marie had told her, of how the situation involved Brigid and Rosie, of how Marie was going to go on living with Leif without ever telling him the truth: 'She's almost out of her mind, Joe–'

He put down his glass; on a coaster, not on the woodwork of the table. 'Are you asking my advice as a lawyer?'

'I dunno. I guess I am–'

He waved his hands in front of him, as if brushing the argument aside. 'As a lawyer, I'd advise her to go to the police. If it was an accident–'

'That's it – it wasn't. Marie hauled off, she said, and hit her on the chin – the slut fell back and cracked her head–'

'You've called her a slut, but what was Leif doing there? Doing charity work? I've suspected for a long time that he might play around–'

She felt a huge clot of guilt flow through her but she couldn't let it out. 'I don't know – maybe he has, but Marie didn't mention it–'

'Leif doesn't know she went to the girl's flat? How long does she think she can keep it from him? Some day, maybe next week, maybe ten years down the track – she's going to have a fight with him, break out and tell him what happened... Jesus, Lou, this is a mess!'

'You think Marie and I don't know it? She's law-abiding, Joe, she's not a criminal. If it weren't for the girls, I know she'd go to the police. But...'

'Yeah. But... Okay, I'm not her lawyer. I want to go and talk to her – does she know you've come to see me?'

'No-o. But I don't think she'll be angry that I have. She is looking for support–'

'We mustn't let Leif know–'

'That's what I told her.' Again guilt hit her.

'I'll go and see her when he's not there – she can tell him it was literary business, I was there as her agent.'

'So many lies – it's going to get complicated–'

He nodded. 'Yeah...' He picked up their glasses. 'You want to go out to eat?'

'No-o. What have you got on hand?'

'My gourmet dinner service girls packed the freezer today. There's a new steak pie, some three-veg combination, orange syrup cake–'

'God, is this how bachelors live?' She stood up, looked at the wall where the pike hung, like a dagger at – whose heart? 'Is that what your dad used in *his* trade?'

He grinned. 'Bullfighting is much more direct than the law. Yeah, that was his. And the saddle, it belonged to a picador who rode for Juan Belmonte. Dad had his idols. Still does, though now they're footballers.'

'You never had those–' She nodded at the pike and the saddle. 'Not when we were–'

'No. Dad had them in storage. When I moved in here, he thought an old-fashioned place like this was just where his idols should be remembered.'

'Have you any idols?' She wondered why her question was so tentative.

Still smiling, he said, 'Only you.'

She smiled in return, shook her head. 'I'm clay up as far as the knees.'

It was a good note on which they went into the kitchen, he to put their dinner in the microwave, she to set the table and look for a bottle of wine. It was a reminder of another time.

They ate, then washed up, he washing, she drying: a domestic scene. When she went into the main bedroom to get her coat, she looked at the big bed, at the four polished posts holding up the fringed canopy.

'Where'd you get it?'

'They were selling up a property down in the Riverina – the family had been there since God knew when. I went down and bought it, had it done up and put that new canopy on it. The guy who did it thought I was Bluebeard. You wanna try it?'

'Not tonight, Joseph,' she said, smiled and took his hand and they went out and down the stairs and out to his car. He drove her home, saying very little to each other, relaxed as an old married couple. He drew up outside her block of flats, switched off the engine and said, 'I'll go and see Marie tomorrow.'

'Treat her gently–'

'I will.' Then he leaned across and kissed

her on the cheek. 'Any regrets?'

Only how I betrayed Marie. 'No. But don't let's rush it. Give me time.'

She went inside and to bed, glad that she had a rock to hold on to.

Chapter Eighteen

1

Marie was well again, sooner than usual; and wished she wasn't. She and Leif made love three and four times a week. Their lovemaking, she had read, was better than the national average; higher pay and longer working hours had reduced the national libido. After the interruption each month, because she was fastidious about hygiene, they would resume like newlyweds. Now, this time, the urge wasn't there for her. She had not become frigid, just frightened.

She even had the bizarre idea of keeping the girls up late, on the pretext that they would hear the evil act. *Evil act? What the hell am I thinking?* She was only experiencing what countless women had: having sex with a husband for whom they no longer had any feelings. But that was the trouble: she did have feelings for him, she still loved him, the bastard.

He came home, looking and saying he was

tired; which she hoped was a sign of temporary escape. He kissed her, went into the living room and hugged the girls, who were looking at *Neighbours*, then came back into the kitchen. It was a large, old-fashioned kitchen and they did not get in each other's way; she was trying to avoid him. He took a beer from the refrigerator, leaned his bum against the draining-board and opened the can.

'How are you feeling?' He sounded genuinely concerned for her.

'Better... Joe was here today.'

'Another book contract?'

'No, just some tidying up on the ones we have.' She was practising being a liar; she would have to be one, even if a silent one, far into the future. 'How are things at the office?'

'Hectic. We haven't a clue what we're supposed to be doing, but we're rushing around like blue-arsed flies. We're novices at this game of how to counter terrorism. Steve Perkins is out of his depth, this is much different from union and faction stoushes. And I'm no better. What do I know about invisible enemies? In politics you always know where the enemy is, on the other side of the House or in your own ranks.'

For a moment she felt a tenderness for him; he was looking for comfort. Almost of its own volition, a gesture of habit, her hand reached out and pressed his arm. 'You'll get better at it–'

He smiled sourly, took a sip of his beer. 'Get better at what? How to recognize an unidentified terrorist? I joke about it–' He was suddenly serious, concerned: 'But I worry about it, too, love. You and the girls, somewhere, some day–'

She was touched. 'Go in and talk to them. Dinner will be another twenty minutes–'

'How's Brigid? She over her pneumonia?'

'Miraculous recovery. She thinks she's got amnesia now – says she can't remember how to spell it.'

He grinned, kissed her again and went in to the girls. *I love him, bugger him.*

She had been surprised when Joe rang her just before lunchtime, had felt annoyed and yet relieved. Louise had obviously spoken to him. She had greeted him at the front door with a kiss and said, 'Are you here as my agent or my lawyer?'

'No, I'm here as your brother-in-law who knows something about the law.'

She led him out to the kitchen where she had prepared soup and toasted sandwiches for lunch. The daily routine had kept her on the rails; kitchens can be therapy rooms. 'I could write a book about this—'

'No, you couldn't.' There was a determined air about him, as if he had been girding himself on the way over. 'And don't ever try it.' They sat down to eat and he said at once, 'Tell me your version of what happened. And don't bullshit me, Mar. Tell me straight.'

She told him, every moment vivid in memory. 'It was an accident, Joe, and yet it wasn't – I *meant* to hurt her, but not to kill her—'

'If ever the police cotton on to you, you'll be charged.' He sipped his soup. 'This is nice – homemade...? Marie, you've got every reason in the world to keep your mouth shut. That goes for Leif as well as the police. And I shouldn't be advising you on those lines – except in the case of Leif. What reaction has he had? He'd have heard or read about it.'

'The police came to see him, but only as her boss, he said—' The soup was tasteless in her mouth. 'Joe, how do I live with it? I hate violence – and look at what I've done—'

'As Lou has told you – you're not alone in this. You keep your mouth shut, unless...' He took another spoonful of soup.

His deliberation annoyed her; yet she knew he was some sort of anchor. 'Unless what?'

'Unless, somehow, the police charge someone else with her death. That's when I start representing you as your lawyer, not as your brother-in-law.'

'Oh, God, that couldn't happen!' She dropped her spoon, ignored it. 'Could it?'

'I don't know, Mar. We don't know how many men this Dinah had, how many wives, like you, were deceived. The police won't let it die – it may be put in the too-hard basket, but it'll always *be* there, to be reopened some time down the track. There are a coupla cases right now, I've been reading about them, that have been dormant for four, five years – they're being reopened. It happens, Mar.'

'You mean I'm going to have this hanging over my head for years?'

'Not necessarily. It depends how you come to accept it. How you come to accept Leif and his affair with this girl. I see it often – not the girl being killed–'

'Don't!'

'Sorry... I see it, the wife accepting or not accepting her husband playing around with another woman. Oddly enough, it's the older wives who accept it, just to hang on to their marriages. You younger ones don't...

280

How are you coping?'

'Not very well.' She picked up her spoon, sipped some soup, now almost cold. Shifted the focus: 'How's it with you and Louise?'

He took his time, bit into one of the sandwiches. 'Smoked salmon – you haven't lost your touch... I'm not sure. Sometimes, for a moment or two, we're *married*. But then... I dunno whether she's afraid of commitment or what. Right now all she's got on her mind is you.'

'She's a great help... You'd take her back?'

He nodded. 'But it's not a question of my taking *her* back. She'd have to take me back. And right now...' He shrugged, chewed on the sandwich, then said, 'Have you taken Leif back?'

'What d'you mean?'

'You know what I mean. I've lived in a marriage bed – I know what it's like...'

'Jesus, is there anything you lawyers don't ask?' He sat silent, taking another mouthful of sandwich, and after a moment she went on, 'Yes ... God, what a subject to be having over lunch!'

'Sorry... Are your publishers still at you to go on a promotion tour?'

'Ye-es. They want me to go to Brisbane, Adelaide and Perth. I'd be away five days.'

'Do it. Get someone to look after the girls and go.'

She looked at him, managed a smile. 'You should've been a woman, Joe.'

'No thanks. You're all far too bloody complicated.'

Then Joe had left and she had gone back to the routine of the day. She had collected the girls from school, picked up Leif's suit in which she had found Dinah's earring, come home and started to prepare dinner. Several fan letters had already arrived and her editor had warned her that shoals more might come surfing in. She answered five of the letters and wondered how she would manage the dozens or hundreds more that would come along. She wondered how Joanne Rowling coped with the thousands and thousands of letters that must come to her. Probably used some Harry Potter magic...

Dinner was pleasantly routine; she was gradually sliding back into gear. The girls chattered, as they always did, and she listened to them and did not tell them to be quiet. Brigid looked at her at one point and said, 'You're in a good mood again.'

'It comes and goes. How's the amnesia?'

'I think I've got whatever she's got,' said Rosie.

'What?' asked Leif.

'I dunno. But I've got it – it's catching–'

Leif put them through their showers and into bed, then came out to the kitchen where she was drying the last of the dishes. Casually, drying a plate, she said, 'My editor wants me to do a five-day author tour. Brisbane, Adelaide and Perth.'

Surprisingly he made no objection: 'I can't go with you. I'm too tied up at the moment. What about the girls?'

The ground was firmer than she had expected; she took another step: 'Would your mother come up and look after them?'

'We could ask her. It'd be a break for her. She says Dad, though he's not on the land, worries all the time about the drought.'

'I thought it had broken–'

'Only in parts of the bush...' Then, almost too casually, he said, 'Jill Bessemer and I have to go to Dinah Camplin's cremation Thursday morning.'

She stopped wiping the forks and knives she had just picked up. 'Why you?'

'She worked for us for two years – I didn't realize she'd been with us that long. The girls in the office have bought a wreath. They suggested Jill and I represent them. I'll sit in a back pew and let Jill give the condolences. Women are better at that.'

'Yes, I guess we are... Have the police been back to you?' She began drying the cutlery.

'No, and I don't expect them back. They seemed satisfied with what they'd got in the office. It's a tragedy,' he said, and shook his head.

'Yes,' she said and put the cutlery away in the drawer, like an assassin waiting for another day. 'Well, shall we ask your mother about coming up?'

'You want to go on this tour?' He looked at her as if all he wanted was what she wanted.

'Not really. I'm not used to it – I don't know how to handle praise, I dunno whether to be smug or modest or what–'

'Be yourself,' he said and kissed the top of her head.

They watched television for an hour or two, a Swedish movie on cable in which there was more nudity than furniture: the sex seemed to take place in rooms that appeared to have nothing in them but beds.

'The Swedes are always at it,' said Leif. 'It must be their overheated houses.'

'In that last scene they were swimming in ice-cold lakes–'

'Yeah, everything looked shrivelled up,' he said and smiled and put his arm round her and kissed her ear.

Oh, God, she thought, why couldn't we have looked at a documentary or the religious channel? They went to bed and were no sooner under the blankets than he reached for her. There was a momentary stiffness to her, then slowly she yielded. She kept her eyes wide open and her mind wide shut and it was as good as usual. But she felt she had betrayed herself.

2

Marie rang Leif's mother and Maeve Johnson said, 'I'd love to, Marie. I'll take them shopping and spend some money on them,' as if her daughter-in-law clothed her family at the Smith Family or St Vincent de Paul.

'They'll love that, Maeve. Brigid is already into the latest fashions—'

'You spoil them, Marie.'

'Yes, I guess I do.' Then, tentatively, wondering what Leif had been like as a boy, she said, 'Didn't you spoil Leif?'

There was silence at the other end of the line for a long moment, then: 'I guess I did. He was my only one—'

She hung up, feeling closer to Leif's

mother than she had ever felt before. Then she rang Biddy Grant at her publishers and said she was all set for the publicity tour.

'Great!' said Biddy, who knew that authors could be harder to handle than children. 'We leave first thing Monday morning. Wear your best – we've got to impress the parents and the grandparents as much as the kids. I'll be in touch–'

Thursday Leif went to Dinah Camplin's cremation out at Rookwood. He came home late and Marie said, 'Where have you been?'

'With the boss and the Premier. I went to the cremation and when we got back they were waiting for me. Steve Perkins and I've been working all afternoon. Canberra is banging the terrorist drum and we're to go down there tomorrow.'

'Just for the day?' He nodded. 'How'd the funeral go?'

'Just like any funeral, I guess. There was quite a crowd, all very well-dressed. Jill did the condolences.' Then he said, almost too casually, 'She had an ex-partner, he was there and said a few words. The police were there, too. When we left, he was going some-where with them–'

Marie felt suddenly cold.

Chapter Nineteen

1

Leif and Jill Bessemer had sat in the very back pew, just inside the doors. The chapel was not large and almost every seat was occupied. The coffin stood on a trestle in front of curtains; soon Dinah would disappear behind the curtains and for a moment everyone would hear the soft roar of the flames. Leif, looking for distraction, wondered why cremation suggested the fires of hell. Was everyone a sinner bound for hell, unless there was a sidetrack somewhere down the line?

On either side of the coffin were banks of wreaths and flowers and Leif tried to remember if Dinah had liked flowers; he had never taken her any, but then he had never been a flower man. The mourners were all well and formally dressed; no one was in sweaters or jeans. Dinah's parents sat side by side in a front pew. Her mother, as Leif had noted when she entered the chapel, was a good-looking woman with a resemblance to Dinah. Her father was a solidly built man with iron-grey hair and a face that had weathered floods, storms and drought. They, and some of the other mourners, were Old Australia, a breed that was dying slowly but inevitably.

A man had approached the lectern and was saying something that Leif didn't catch. 'Who's he?'

'Haven't a clue,' whispered Jill.

A woman in front of them turned and also whispered, 'He's Dinah's ex-partner. They were very close.'

Leif looked at the man: the *possessive* ex-partner. Could he have–? But Leif shook the thought out of his mind. The man was about Leif's age, slimly built with a handsome face and balding hair cut to a shadow. He spoke in a low voice and appeared genuinely grief-stricken. Leif felt nothing for him. None of these people, the mourners, Leif realized with a shock of shame, had played any part in his relationship with Dinah.

He looked around the chapel, then glanced across at the back pew on the other side of the aisle. Detectives Mendez and Stephen sat there, faces frozen, strangers like himself at the gathering. Then Mendez looked across at him and nodded, as if he had expected Leif to be there. Leif felt a sudden coldness, as if he had forgotten that Dinah had been murdered and Mendez and Stephen were there to remind him.

At last the service was over. The curtains slid back and the coffin moved slowly back into the waiting flames. Dinah was gone and up front someone let out a sob.

'I'll meet you outside,' Jill whispered. 'I'll speak to her parents.'

Leif got up, moving stiffly, and went out into the cold bright sunshine. He stood to one side of the path, looking around him, cold inside from more than just the wind from the south. The mourners spilled out, slowly, as if witnessing death had aged them. Then Mendez was beside him:

'I didn't expect you here, Mr Johnson.'

'I'm here with my 2 i/c. The office donated a wreath and Miz Bessemer and I are here representing them.' Even in his own ears he sounded formal, as if Mendez, like a traffic cop, was about to give him a ticket. 'Why are you here?'

'We're still on our enquiries. Oh, excuse me–'

He abruptly tuned away, walked across to Stephen, who had just come out of the

289

chapel with Dinah's ex-partner. There was a short conversation, then the three of them walked away towards the line of parked cars, the ex-partner between the two police officers.

Was he a suspect? Then Leif turned as Jill Bessemer came out of the chapel. He looked at her as he might have at a stranger. She wore a black trouser suit, white sweater and a black beret; she looked impregnable, he thought, safe against the world and, for the moment, the fires of hell. He admired her strength and wondered where his own had gone.

'Okay, we can go,' she said briskly. 'We've paid our respects.'

'What are her parents like?' You sleep with a woman and know nothing of her beyond her flesh and only some parts of her mind.

'Nice, old-fashioned, polite. But shattered... I hate funerals.' They began to walk back to Leif's car. 'Hate 'em,' she said, as if she had been attending them all her life.

'Did you listen to the tributes?' He opened the doors of the Volvo and they got in. 'I didn't know her that well–' he lied. *Or had he?* 'But could she have been that good? Mother Teresa?'

'Leif, funerals are for homage, not honesty.

I dunno about Dinah, but if mourners spoke the truth at most funerals, the undertakers would be running ambulances as well as hearses.'

'You're so bloody cynical–'

'It helps make staying alive bearable.'

He looked at her, wondering what blight and disappointment she had had, but he said nothing. He started up the car and drove away from Dinah Camplin.

2

Leif went down to Canberra with Steve Perkins. Security checking at the airport was perfunctory and he made a note for Perkins to bring it up at the conference. A government car was waiting for them at Canberra airport and they were driven through a cold day and a wind that came down from the snow-topped surrounding ranges. The many trees of the capital were bare, their branches outstretched like the arms of semaphorists waiting to be told what messages to send. The car drew up outside a government building, white and cold as an ice-house. Leif came to Canberra only rarely and was always glad to leave it. He had twice resisted offers to come and work here.

The conference was cordial, no politics involved, but vague. Terrorism was still only a concept for this nation at, as a Prime Minister had once described it, the arse-end of the world. The voters knew only images: huge buildings crashing to the ground in a thunderstorm of smoke and dust, a shattered red bus, mangled corpses in a Baghdad gutter. Leif had once seen a movie on television about a boy who lived in a glass or plastic bubble. Australia was living in a bubble.

In the plane going back to Sydney, Steve Perkins said, 'Well, what did you think?'

'We're not even at the starting gate yet – but don't quote me. I'll dream up some bullshit and make us look as if we've achieved something.'

Perkins nodded and smiled. 'What would we do without you spin-doctors...? You only learn from experience, so they say. Let's hope we never experience it... I believe you went to that girl's funeral yesterday, the one who worked for us and was murdered?'

The remark brought Leif back to the real world. 'Jill Bessemer and I went, representing the office.'

'I saw her around a coupla times. She was

a good sort. Pity she had to go like that –
there's too much bloody violence these days.
They any idea who killed her? I understand
the police came to see you.' Steve Perkins, an
old union boss, never missed much. Maybe
they should make him head of ASIO,
thought Leif.

'Routine enquiries, they said.' How far into
the future would he be reminded of Dinah?

'I wonder how soon we'll be making
routine enquiries about terrorists?'

'Let's hope never.'

Friday night and all day Saturday Leif was
as close to Marie as he had been when they
first married; he *needed* her, though he did
not think in those terms. There was a
reliability about her that he had taken for
granted, that he now found he needed.

His mother came up from Cowra on Sunday, driving her own Land Rover, as efficient
and bossy as ever. She was a tall buxom
woman with good looks that she had be-
queathed to Leif; she was a leader, had been
all her life. Girl Guides, women's rights,
countrywomen's committees: the world had
to be organized.

She kissed him, hugged the girls, then
turned to Marie: 'You're right. Let's spoil
'em, all three of them.'

Leif looked at his wife and his mother: 'What's with it with you two?'

Marie gave him what he had once called one of her mystery smiles. 'Mothers' talk. You wouldn't understand.'

Probably not. Over the past week or so he had come to realize how far short he was in education: about women, a subject as complicated and vague as history itself.

Chapter Twenty

1

From the moment that Leif told her that Dinah Camplin's ex-partner had been taken away for questioning by the police, Marie lived on the edge of panic. Friday morning, after Leif had left for Canberra, she scanned the morning newspapers; Leif had all four delivered, went through them, then left them at home when he went to the office. There was nothing about 'a man helping with enquiries', but that didn't mean the ex-partner was off the hook. At lunchtime she rang Joe.

'I'm worried stiff, Joe. Leif was at her funeral yesterday. He saw the police taking away her ex-partner–'

'Relax, Mar–' He was answering her on his mobile. He had told her not to call him on the office switch; he did not suspect that Shanyne listened in to calls, but one could never be sure that the line was not accidentally left open. 'They do it all the time–'

'But what if they charge him?' She had seen too many crime series on television. The world of crime was framed by *Law & Order*.

'Then you and I have another talk. Take it easy, Mar, or you're going to have a nervous breakdown. Call me again on Monday.'

'I'm going to Brisbane–'

'Okay, so go. And enjoy it.'

'That's easy for you to say–'

'No, it's not. And don't you ever think it.'

She enjoyed the weekend with Leif and the girls; it was like old times. *Old times:* a week, ten days ago. She liked Maeve being with them Sunday evening, as if she had discovered a new friend. Sunday night they did not make love, aware of ears in another room, older than Brigid's and Rosie's. Monday morning she woke, furtively searched the newspapers, but there was nothing. Only bad news for other people.

She flew to Brisbane, ignored by the airline staff. She was just another passenger; they were obviously illiterate, never read books.

'Get used to it,' said Biddy Grant. 'Authors are hoi-polloi outside of bookstores and writers' festivals.'

Once back on the ground, Marie had a

hectic day: signed books, was interviewed, photographed. She was exhausted by it all and was glad that Biddy called off a dinner with the publishers' two local sales reps. She and Biddy had dinner at the hotel, then retreated to Marie's suite for a nightcap.

'Champagne?' The hotel's management had left half a bottle and some crackers and cheese. 'I usually don't drink before going to bed.'

'Make the most of it,' said Biddy.

'You don't think all this will last?'

Biddy, lolling in a chair, looked at her. 'Marie, I've been in this game ten years next month. I've been frozen out by some authors, groped by others – I'm a closer student of authors than any literary critic. You'd be surprised the number of authors who don't last. You'll last, I'm sure – and I'm not peeing in your pocket.'

'I still haven't any idea what next to write–'

'It'll come.'

Marie, glass in hand, sat down opposite her, curled her legs under her. 'Do you have a boyfriend? A partner?'

'Three of them.'

'Three? Boyfriends or partners?'

'I look on them as partners–'

Marie hid her surprise. 'You live – what do they call it? – *ménage-à-quatre?*'

Biddy had the cheeky grin of a wayward schoolgirl. 'I don't *live* with any of them. And none of them knows about the others.'

'God, you should be writing *Bridget Jones' Diary!* And you don't feel–?' She didn't want to use the word, she liked Biddy too much.

'Promiscuous? Yes, sometimes. I want to get married, be like you, have a husband I love and a coupla children, maybe more... I'm living dangerously, getting too old for it – I'm thirty-two–'

'My age. I thought you were younger. Three partners must keep you youthful.'

'You're kidding. I'm ageing by the minute. Be glad and happy with what you've got, your husband – he's nice – and your girls.'

'I'll try–'

They moved on from Brisbane to Adelaide and Perth, foreign cities for Marie; she had travelled abroad, but knew little of her own country beyond Sydney. The tour was as successful in the other two cities as it had been in Brisbane; Barney Guinness would never, ever, be as popular as Harry Potter, but he was building his own voters. Bank robbery, even by kids with a gift for larceny, was replacing magic as entertainment. It was, as Biddy Grant remarked, a sign of the times. The directors of Enron and Worldcom and HIH were the new Brothers Grimm.

Each morning Marie borrowed Biddy's laptop, on the pretext that she was checking if Leif's press releases on terrorism were getting any spread. But, online, she raced through each of the Sydney newspapers for any item, no matter how brief, on whether a man was being held for questioning on the death of Dinah Camplin. But there was nothing.

She returned to Sydney Friday night. Leif came to the airport to meet her, greeted her as if she had been away for five months rather than five days.

'He misses me,' she told Biddy. 'Let me know how your three greet you.'

'Her three?' said Leif as he and Marie drove out of the airport parking lot, having just paid a ransom for his car's release. 'Her kids?'

'No, her partners. She believes in safety in numbers. How are Brigid and Rosie?'

'Delirious. Mum has spoiled them blind.'

She looked at him, loving him, feeling safe for the moment. That was how the future might be, moment by moment, but she would weather it.

She wondered if one could write a love story for children.

2

Joe was having another session with Sophie Purdell and her mother:

'Jamie's parents have been in touch – they want to withdraw all charges.'

'Can they do that?' asked Sophie, prim and proper in her school uniform.

'Why? Don't you want them to?'

'I want everyone to know what a bastard he is.'

Oh, the venom of women! Joe wasn't sure who had written that, but it had to be a man. 'The DPP, the Director of Public Prosecutions, may still go ahead with it–'

'It's his parents,' said Mrs Purdell, secure today in navy blue, expensively cut, crocodile-skin bag discarded in favour of a Vuitton saddlebag; Joe couldn't see her feet, but he knew she wouldn't be wearing trainers. 'Jamie's father, he's afraid of what they'll say to him at his clubs.'

'Sophie–' Joe was patient. 'Do you want your baby born in gaol?'

For a moment there was a crack in the

primness. 'Well, no-o...'

'We'll see what the DPP intends–' He looked at Mrs Purdell; there was no crack in her elegance. 'Let Jamie's father prevail. If they drop the charges, but the DPP goes ahead and Sophie goes to gaol, who wins?'

The mother reached across and pressed her daughter's arm. Joe, looking at them, knew this sort of thing was not supposed to happen in their circle; this was what happened to the unseen poor, the people they read about, it didn't happen to them. But it had and, looking at them, Joe knew the two would survive.

'Mr Fernandez is right, sweetheart–'

'No,' said Joe. 'I'm not right. There are no winners in this. Except your baby, Sophie – we hope.'

The girl hesitated, then she nodded. 'How do you know so much?'

He shook his head, gave his small smile. 'Guesswork, Sophie. And some mixed experience. Good luck.'

The girl and her mother left, walking out the door, he thought, to a side street of life they had never envisaged. He wondered if Sophie still had her hockey stick.

Then Edith came into his office. 'She happy?'

'No-o. Why does revenge taste so sweet? It should be the sourest taste there is.'

'It sometimes is,' said Edith, but didn't elaborate, just turned and went out of the room. And for the first time he wondered what secrets *she* had.

He sat for a while, mind blank; he had the trick of being able to do that, to stop thinking. Then he came back into gear, picked up his mobile and called Marie.

'How are you coping?'

'Still biting my nails.'

'How's it with Leif? You know what I mean—'

'God, what are you – a lawyer or a gynaecologist? It's okay.'

'Just okay?'

'There you go – no, it's better than okay. That satisfy you?'

'Good – but don't get snarly with me, love. Now I'd like to come to dinner—'

'What? And watch Leif and me?'

'Don't be crude, Mrs Johnson. No, to give you a rundown on how things are going. I don't think there'll be any more offers for *Barney*, unless they come from Uzbekistan or Afghanistan – no, forget Afghanistan. The warlords there could learn nothing from kid bank robbers.'

He clicked off the mobile, sat staring at the shelves of books opposite him but not seeing them. He felt suddenly terribly lonely, as if surrounded by an empty world. Which, even as he thought it, he knew wasn't true. The world was full of pain and hunger and all the ills of history. You had to search for joy, but he knew it was there. Somewhere.

3

Louise had had another bad week on the Chapelli counter. Luxury buying, it seemed, was out; but then, it also seemed, nobody was buying anything. It had been a warm winter and in other departments at Dampiers winter stock was still on the shelves and racks. Mira had reported from menswear that the chances of inside-leg measurements had vanished. Oil prices were still rising and the world economy was darkening. On the other side of the world a hurricane named Katrina (why were the worst storms always named after women? Why hadn't they called it Hurricane George?) was approaching Louisiana and down in New Orleans Bourbon Street looked like being diluted with water. The war in Iraq was a stalemate,

Europe was a flaky cake, and millions still, as ever, were starving in Africa. The Rolling Stones, looking like cracked effigies, were making another tour. The world was going backwards, Louise decided, and sprayed her wrists, instead of cutting them, with perfume from a sample bottle.

She had not seen Marie in two weeks, but their discreet phone calls to each other had shown that Marie was coping, if only just.

'I've closed my eyes, metaphorically,' said Marie, 'and everything is okay with Leif.'

'Metaphorically? I must try that some time with–' But then she stopped.

'Who with? Joe?'

'No, not with him. I've got my eyes wide open there.'

'Take him back, Lou–'

'What if he won't take *me* back? It's easy for you to talk–' Then she stopped and laughed, dryly. 'You said that to me a while ago–'

'My conscience still worries me.'

'Conscience makes cowards of us all – I dunno who said that–'

'Shakespeare, *Hamlet*,' said Marie, who was better-read and had the better memory. 'We did an amateur production my last year at uni. I was Ophelia, remember?'

Louise laughed. 'I remember – you were bloody awful... Hang in there, Mar. Keep your eyes shut, metaphorically. Give my love to the girls.'

She had dinner twice with Joe, but the dates did not lead to bed. She kissed him goodnight, let him feel her breasts, but then put up a Stop sign. 'Give me more time, Joe,' she said. 'I'm still playing goalie for Marie.'

'You've never played sport in your life–'

'No, but I've watched Brigid and Rosie playing soccer. I know what has to be kept out.'

'You're not keeping Leif out of her bed, are you? For Crissake!'

'No, nothing like that. In fact, I'm advising the reverse–'

He had sat back from her, nodded. 'Yeah, but she's got to manage that on her own... As for you and me – I'm a patient man.'

'Your bloody patience used to drive me up the wall–' But she smiled as she said it; she kissed him again, opened the door of his car. 'Let's be patient, Joe.'

Rob Loomis called her and asked her to dinner, but she declined.

'Have I worn out my welcome?' he asked. 'Or are you disappointed in me?'

'Neither, Rob. You were a friend and comfort when I needed it–'

'And I'm not that any more?' He sounded hurt.

She said hurriedly, still feeling affection, but not love, for him: 'You still are, Rob – truly. But–' She hesitated, then decided he was a man she could confide in: 'I'm seeing my ex-husband again–'

'Good. I always had the feeling you'd never entirely forgotten him.'

She was surprised. 'Was it that obvious?'

'I'm a sensitive guy, Louise–' He laughed. 'Wasn't that why you and I got along so well?'

'Some day I'd like you to meet him–'

'That wouldn't be wise. Good luck, darling.' And he hung up abruptly and she wondered if emotion had hit him. It would not be because she had hurt him, but because he had had no luck himself. She felt terribly sad for him.

A couple of nights later she rang Joe. 'We're going up to see my father Saturday. Your parents are coming down to him and Marie is shouting us lunch. You want to come?'

'Mum and Dad have already been in touch. I'll pick you up. How are you?'

She thought about it, then said, 'Relaxed.

Except about Marie.'

'She's bearing up. On paper she's just made her first million.'

'Are you taking any of it as her agent?'

'Ten per cent.'

'You thieving bastard!'

'That's all most men get out of any woman,' he said and hung up laughing.

4

Leif and Marie were on the Warringah expressway, heading north in the Volvo. Brigid and Rosie, torn between soccer and its lovely mayhem and a day out on Pa Micklethwaite's beach, were strapped in the back seat and complaining why did car trips always take so long.

'Pull your head in,' said Marie; it was a family saying. 'You wouldn't complain if a treasure was buried at the end of the trip.'

'Is it?' said Rosie and looked at her sister.

'You know what she's like,' said Brigid, as if their mother was a kilometre ahead of them in another car. 'She's a *writer*.'

'Yeah,' said Rosie and nodded her head as if the future was bleak.

Leif looked at Marie and grinned. 'Homegrown literary critics.'

He was surprised how, over the last couple of weeks, he had become so relieved and relaxed. The shadow of Dinah's death had passed; the police had not been back to him. The ex-partner evidently was no longer under suspicion; it looked more and more like she had been killed by 'person or persons unknown'. He still felt guilt about his association with her; but the tragedy had brought him hard up against a brick wall, one he would never climb again. Conscience bit at him again each time he saw Louise, but she had erected her own wall between them and he knew the subject would never be raised. Now, in the car, he looked at Marie and smiled, safe and happy and unbelievably lucky.

'What are you smiling at?'

'You three, you and the two know-alls in the back.'

She smiled in return, touched his arm, and Brigid in the back yelped, 'Don't touch him! He's driving!'

'Pull your head in,' said Marie again; then to Leif: 'That conference you had yesterday – there was nothing about it in any of the papers.'

'It was buried on page six in the *Herald*.' It

had been a small conference of security experts, presided over by Steve Perkins, an expert on nothing but party politics. 'Hurricane Katrina got all the space. People forget that the biggest terrorist of all is nature.'

'Did your conference achieve anything?'

'Bugger-all. We're about as coordinated as Brigid's soccer team.'

Brigid opened her mouth to protest, but Marie, looking back at her, said, 'Pull your head in.'

'I'm so bloody lucky,' said Leif to the world at large.

'You certainly are,' said Marie. 'Isn't he, girls?'

The girls just shrugged, pulling their heads in.

Chapter Twenty-One

1

'Doc Teddes is still with us, floundering around,' said Matt Micklethwaite. 'Doesn't know his arse from his elbow.'

'You're swearing again, Pa,' said Rosie.

'No, I'm not, love. Arse is now a polite word with politicians and rock stars and what used to be called nice young ladies. But if ever I hear you using it, I'll cut you out of my will.'

'Your will?' said Brigid. 'What's that?'

'My plumber's tool kit and a dollar ninety-five in the bank.' Then he looked at Marie, grinned and sucked on a lobster claw. 'Nice lunch, Mar.'

Marie, mad with money, had ordered lobster and champagne for lunch; the bill would render American Expressionless. The restaurant was opposite the beach and out beyond the sands the surf rose up like white-vined walls on which rode four or five wet-suited surfers like leaping black marlin.

A mild wind blew from the south and the sky had only small graffiti of clouds streaking it. Gulls stood on the wind, white apostrophes on the blue page.

'My father used to catch *langosta* off Benidorm – he was a fisherman,' said Hernando. 'They were smaller than these.'

'There would be none there now,' said Isabella, and Louise, observing them both, was once again aware that Joe's parents still clung to what once had been.

Joe, napkin to chin, a piece of lobster skewered on a fork, said, 'The best seafood in the world is here in Australia.'

Isabella looked at Hernando and said, 'We should of left him in Benidorm,' and everyone laughed.

Louise covertly looked around the table. There was happiness here; not a care hung in the air. She was sitting between Brigid and Rosie, who were bogging into the lobster with no thought of decorum; for all the gourmets' conceit, she thought, children and savages are the best enjoyers of food. She raised her champagne glass: 'Here's to all of us. But most of all to Rosie and Brigid.' Out of the corner of her eye she watched Leif and Marie, but both were bland and happy behind their raised glasses. 'And to Dr Teddes–'

'Bugger,' said Matt. 'My bloody champagne has just turned sour.'

'Pa–' said Brigid.

'Pull your head in,' said her grandfather and they both laughed, the same age for the moment.

Later Louise and Marie went for a walk along the beach. The wind had strengthened, but was no colder. The surf had risen even further and the surfers, only three of them now, seemed to hang in the air. Louise and Marie pulled up their coat collars and walked arm in arm. Then they came to a halt, half a kilometre from the restaurant, beyond earshot.

'I looked at you and Leif today,' said Louise. 'Everything looks okay, on the surface.'

'Better than that,' said Marie, the wind whipping her hair about her face. 'It's just like it used to be–'

'Keep it up–'

'But–' Marie looked out to sea; the clouds had started to thicken, but were not threatening. 'It's going to be a long haul, Lou. Will I ever tell him what I did? What I know?'

'No,' said Louise, as if it were her decision alone. 'I looked at Brigid and Rosie again today. They're your future. Just remember that.'

'The funny thing is, I think I love him more than ever – as if I've won him back. And he feels the same way – I think.'

'I think so, too. I was watching him.'

Marie smiled. 'I was watching you, too. You're still – or once again – in love with Joe.'

The wind caught at the corners of Louise's eyes; for a moment there were tears there. 'Yes. I'm going to ask him to marry me again.'

'Oh, Lou!'

The sisters hugged each other, close as twins, and down on the beach the three surfers, coming out of the water, stopped and stared.

'Holy shit, look at those two dykes groping each other in public! You'd think they'd wait till they got home!'

The rest of the world looks at strangers through cracked bifocals.

2

Driving back to Sydney Louise said, 'Can you feed me this evening? Something light?'

Joe, a man who drove with concentration, relaxed for the moment, glanced at her. 'There's nothing in the freezer. How do you fancy some fish and chips, we can pick some up? I've got a bottle of Bollinger to go with them.'

'Fish and chips and French champagne... What was that Roman feast they used to have?'

'Lucullan.'

'Perfect!' She leaned across and kissed his ear and for a moment the BMW wavered in its line.

When they arrived at Strathfield they went up through the darkened lower floors of the mansion, Joe carrying the fish and chips in a plastic bag, the stairs creaking beneath their feet, not as a warning but almost welcoming. Joe switched on all the lights in his flat and Louise stood and looked around.

'It's you, Joe. Old-fashioned, solid and reliable.' Then she looked directly at him, deciding against wasting any more time: 'Will you marry me again?'

'Funny you should mention that–' He moved to her, took her in his arms. 'We've wasted a lot of time, love.'

She nodded and kissed him, hungrily, holding him to her. Then she moved back: 'Let's be domestic. Let's have the fish and chips before they get cold. And then–'

Later, in the big canopied bed, they began

life again. They were alone: outside, the world was empty. Later still, she got out of bed, went into the bathroom, then came back and sat on the side of the bed, Joe's shirt around her shoulders.

'No fuss, okay? We'll be married quietly, in a church, nobody but our families there.'

'Whatever you want.' Then he said, 'I looked at Marie and Leif today. They're happy.'

'But?'

He smiled his small grin. 'You always know when there's a *but*... But can Marie keep her mouth shut for the rest of her life?'

'I think so. For the girls' sake. And her own–' Then she frowned, looking hard at him. 'You still have your doubts–'

'I'm a lawyer, love. I can't help having respect for the law.'

'I'll cure you of that,' she said lightly; but then, serious, leaned forward. 'Darling–' The word was like cream on her tongue. It was not a social affectation nor an endearment for Brigid and Rosie. It was new love for an old lover. 'It's about a family. What would the righteous and the law-abiding have done?'

'I don't know,' said Joe.

Kirribilli
April–September 2005

The publishers hope that this book has given you enjoyable reading. Large Print Books are especially designed to be as easy to see and hold as possible. If you wish a complete list of our books please ask at your local library or write directly to:

Magna Large Print Books
Magna House, Long Preston,
Skipton, North Yorkshire.
BD23 4ND

This Large Print Book, for people
who cannot read normal print,
is published under the auspices of

THE ULVERSCROFT FOUNDATION